CW00538686

Fo
tha
Fa
Co
ha
ar

in
o
h
s
a
c
b
f

The Chickamaugo Covenant

ELLIOT CONWAY

A Black Horse Western

ROBERT HALE · LONDON

© Elliot Conway 1992
First published in Great Britain 1992

ISBN 0 7090 4771 1

Robert Hale Limited
Clerkenwell House
Clerkenwell Green
London EC1R 0HT

The right of Elliot Conway to be identified as
author of this work has been asserted by him
in accordance with the Copyright, Designs and
Patents Act 1988.

For Reg Taylor
and all the help he gave me

491672
F

Photoset in North Wales by
Derek Doyle & Associates, Mold, Clwyd.
Printed in Great Britain by
St Edmundsbury Press, Bury St Edmunds, Suffolk.
Bound by WBC Bookbinders Ltd, Bridgend, Glamorgan.

ONE

The big-framed rider drew up his mount on the ridge, groaning loudly as he ass-shuffled in his saddle in an attempt to ease the pains in his back. He then cast a long look across the flats stretching for miles below him. In the middle distance, blurred in his vision by the shimmering heat waves and dust spirals, he saw what he had come to Texas for. It was a journey the war had prevented him from making for two years and entailed a long trip south from Minnesota, the last two days of it a bone-jarring horse ride. He kneed his horse down the slope and the well-beaten trail that led to the Double Star ranch. Frank Eberhart was fulfilling the promise he had made lying wounded in the bloodletting hell that was known as the battle of Chickamaugo.

Coming closer Frank could make out a double-storeyed main house, several barns and store huts and beyond the ranch buildings, a sizeable herd of beef. He caught the tangy smell of burning hide and heard a calf's squeal of protest as the branding-iron was being applied. His first impression was that the Double Star was a going concern. Widow Isobel Farrow had not let the death of her husband bring ruination on what he must have

5

built up before going off to fight for the Con-
federacy and getting himself killed.

He had come to Texas to help her out; how, he
didn't rightly yet know. If she had moved on or got
herself a new husband, his long trail from Hubbard
County, Minnesota, to Texas would have been all
for nothing. But at least he had honoured part of his
covenant made while lying wounded with the dead
body of Captain Farrow stretched across his legs. He
had made the trip. Frank then thought about how
and when he was going to tell the Widow Farrow
that if her husband had not got off his horse to save
a blue-belly sergeant from being burnt to death in
the brush at Chickamaugo she still might have had a
husband and her boy a pa. Chickamaugo. Frank
shuddered. That bloody corner of hell. He felt the
wounds in his legs twitch painfully as though it had
been only yesterday he had got himself shot. Then
he had been Sergeant Frank Eberhart of the 2nd
Minnesota Volunteers, Company A, the German
and Dutch company, attacking the reb entrenchments before their key communication and
railroad centre, Chattanooga. The company had
been eating dirt behind a railroad cutting waiting
for the next reb counterattack. He still woke up
some nights, shaking and sweating, hearing the
rebel yells as Hood's division of wild-eyed, ragged-
assed Texan veterans came storming out of the
wood.

'Here they come, Sergeant, for the last time.' Major
Kruger grinned what he thought was a reassuring,
confident grin to his top sergeant. 'If we can hold
them this time then by golly we've got them
whupped. We can get up off our bellies and chase

the sonsuvbitches clear back to Chattanooga.'

Major Kruger's grimace didn't look like a coming victory celebration smile to Sergeant Eberhart; more like the expression of a man gripped by bowel pains. Just to hold his squad together he gave them an equally tight-assed grin. 'You heard the major, boys,' he said. 'We've about those southern boys licked. Come nightfall we should be whoopin' it up in Chattanooga drinking real southern whiskey and sampling the friendship of real Southern belles.'

Frank's face hardened at the memory. Most of the boys he had spoke that crap to never saw Chattanooga, never saw but a few more minutes of their lives. The rebs came at them in a seemingly never-ending series of howling, gunfiring, bayonet-jabbing waves. He saw the major, standing on top of the cutting, sword in his hand yelling at the company to stand firm, bloodily swept away as a hail of bullets ripped into him. Then the company broke and it was every man for himself with the rebs howling at their heels like demented hound dogs. Frank found himself clawing his way through a wild tangle of chest-high brush and scrub oaks in full panic when he felt a searing pain in both of his legs and blacked out.

When he regained consciousness the louder noises of the battle had shifted well to his rear. Only faintly could he hear the rattle of musketry fire and bursting cannon shells. Nearer at hand, from the piles of blue and grey uniformed bundles, he heard the real sounds of battle, the cries and the groans of the wounded. And another noise that chilled his blood still further. The crackling and roaring of flames that were sweeping through the underbrush towards him.

Frank painfully turned over on to his stomach and began elbowing his way from the rapidly approaching wall of fire, his legs useless dead weights. Behind him, frantically spurring him on, he heard the agonizing screams of the wounded unable to get out of the fire's path. He got as far as the edge of a clearing then collapsed on his face, too weak to progress any further. Fighting off waves of nausea that threatened to make him black out again he wildly looked round for a discarded weapon, rifle, pistol, bayonet, within hand's reach, determined to put an end to his life rather than suffer being roasted alive, conscious, or unconscious.

Several riders burst into the clearing from his left and in a last desperate effort to escape the hell of the inferno, whose heat he could feel drying the sweat that he had raised crawling, he lifted himself up on to his elbows and shouted for help then dropped face to the dirt again. He thought for several frightening moments his cries had gone unheard when hands gripped his shoulders and sobbing with relief he was dragged well into the clearing. The pain he suffered was a small price to pay for escaping the more fearful agony of being cremated alive. He raised his head to thank his rescuer and his spoken thanks died in his throat as he saw the grey uniform. The reb officer favoured him with a thin smile.

'That's the best I can do for you, Sergeant,' he said, 'Your boys are pressing us back damned hard. They're close on our tails.'

Rifle fire suddenly blazed out across the clearing

from the direction the retreating rebs had appeared and cheering and yelling Union troops poured out of the brush. Frank heard the sickening thud of a Minié ball hitting soft, vulnerable flesh; heard the Confederate officer's sharp intake of breath as with face set in dying lines of pain he collapsed across his legs. Just as quickly the clearing was emptied of the counterattacking troops as they hurtled their way through the trees to straighten out their broken and bent line, leaving only the medical orderlies to tend to the wounded of the earlier fighting.

Two days later, lying on his cot, wounds cleaned and dressed, at a medical clearing station, Frank had time to look at the articles he had taken off the dead reb officer, before some light-fingered Union soldier grabbed them. There were three well-creased letters in the envelope all beginning with *My Darling James* and ending with, *all our love, Isobel and Lee*. Frank didn't read the texts of the letters. He didn't feel he had the right to probe into a dead man's affairs more than he had to.

The envelope was addressed to Captain James Farrow, Company D, 8th Texas Cavalry. On its reverse side was the address of the sender, Double Star ranch, Brazo County, Texas. On opening the case of the gold half-hunter, Frank saw a small tintype photograph of a woman's face, a dark-haired, plumpish, happy face. He snapped the case shut and weighed the watch and its fob in his hand deep in thought. He would see to it that the captain's widow got the watch back, always providing of course he came through this goddamned war alive. He owed the captain that and more. If he had stayed on his horse and let him burn he could have still been alive and writing more letters to his sweet-faced wife, and, he assumed, his boy, Lee. Frank's face hardened in determination. Come hell and high water he was going to make that trip to Brazo County and no piddling little war was going to stop him doing so.

Frank got off the train at a water halt west of Forth Worth. While he was checking over his horse for any injuries it may have suffered in its long spell in a boxcar he asked the driver of a buckboard busy loading crates of merchandise from a rail flatcart on his wagon for directions to the Double Star ranch. The driver, a small, plains-dried husk of a man, pointed northwards.

'Ain't no need tuh travel that fur, stranger,' he said. 'There's three or four cattle-spreads nearer than that tuh try yuhr luck at. It's round-up time; the herds will be trailin' north tuh Kansas and the ranchers will welcome any hombre that can throw his leg over a horse and knows the front end of a cow from its ass.' The old man shook his head sadly. 'Texas grass is black with longhorns, it's the boys that's lackin' tuh drive them north. Half of them that did make it back are so badly shot up they can't get astride a pony.' Black shoe-button eyes hard-fixed Frank in an unblinking stare. 'Yuh sound like a Yankee to me, mister, are yuh?'

Frank swung on to his horse and looked down at the old trader. He grinned. 'Could well be, old timer, could well be. Thanks for your information, and good day to you.' Frank's grin soon vanished, realizing that was something he hadn't really thought about; how kindly would Texans take to an ex-blue-belly showing up asking for work on the

ranch with all those dead southern boys hardly cold
in their graves yet. His pa had hinted that he
should wait awhile before he up and hauled
himself off to Texas. They were sitting on the front
stoop smoking their makings and Frank had felt
that it was time that he told his father what was on
his mind. Mr Eberhart listened in silence to all that
his son was telling him. Before he said his piece he
looked long and hard at him. He didn't want to lose
him so soon. He had hardly been back home six
months. But he knew when Frank made up his
mind to do a thing he just got up and did it.
Half-heartedly he tried to dissuade him from
leaving.

'Things will be still mighty unsettled down there,
boy,' he said. 'The war hasn't been over all that
long. Just send the watch with a letter of
explanation to Mrs Farrow. Then m'be, if she
replies to your letter, or if you still feel that you're
obliged to visit her you can make the trip.'

'No, Pa,' replied Frank firmly. 'I've got to go
now. She could be trying to run the ranch on her
own, m'be getting into debt; I don't know that, but
I won't rest easy till I find out how things really
stand with her. I know that it isn't fair of me
wanting to leave you and Ma after just getting back
from the war. It means that most of the work on
the farm is falling on your shoulders again, Pa. But
I owe Captain Farrow. You and Ma owe him. He
let you have me back.'

Mr Eberhart got to his feet. 'Yes we do owe the
good captain,' he said, sober faced. 'You go to
Texas, boy, and see the widow lady then m'be your
mind will give you some peace so that you can settle
down and think about your own future.' He smiled

at his son. 'I've coped without you being around for the last couple of years so I reckon that a few more weeks managing just with the help of your Ma won't break my back none.'

Frank remembered his father's words as he slow rode up to the bunch of ranch-hands calf branding near the main herd. He was about to find out just how unsettled things were in Texas and what sort of reception an ex-enemy would get. There were five men grouped round a tied-down kicking and squealing calf. The men stopped their work at the sound of his approach. Frank gave them a grin. 'How'de, gents,' he said. 'Mind if I step down and water my horse?'

It was the man holding the branding-iron, a thickset elderly man that answered him. Frank immediately tagged him as straw boss of the Double Star.

'There's water in the trough over beside the barn,' he said. 'You're welcome to help yourself.'

'Thanks,' replied Frank as he dismounted. 'I'm intendin' making my way to New Mexico, got blood kin there I haven't seen since before the war. I thought that m'be I'd get myself a spell of work on some ranch, kinda pay for the expenses of my trip. I heard that the lady that owns this ranch is hiring.'

'You heard right, mister,' the stocky man said, 'Mrs Farrow is hiring men. But I'm doin' the pickin'. I'm Sam Ford, foreman of the Double Star. Just because the ranch wants men it don't mean that we take on any asshole of a drifter that shows up hoping that he can swing himself a free meal and feed for his horse pretending he is what he ain't. Do you know anything about herding cattle, mister?'

Frank gave an inner sigh of relief. Mrs Farrow still owned the ranch. So far it had not been a wasted journey. Before he could tell the ranch foreman that he could handle the general chores on a ranch a narrow-shouldered youth with a black patch over his left eye and his shirt pinned up over the stump of his left arm said, 'You smell like a damn Yankee to me, mister.' The single eye glared fiercely at him from an old man's face.

Frank gave him a smile. 'You're the second fella that's asked me that question in the last couple days.' His smile began to fade as he saw the youth's hand reaching towards the pistol sheathed low on his right hip. 'I don't wear a gun right now,' he said, 'so I can't stop you for shooting me down like a dog. I don't know about Texas but where I come from that kinda shootin's classed as murder. If you're that keen to get what's eatin' at your insides out of your system then face me like a man in a fist fight.' Frank thin-smiled him. 'Then m'be I'll be guilty of murder for the way the war's left you it'll be no trouble at all for me to beat the hell outa you. So why don't you back off, kid, and let me water my horse! Haven't you witnessed enough killing to want to hanker for more?'

'Yeah, you do just that, Phil,' the Double Star foreman growled. 'You're taking the boss lady's money to herd cattle. It's as the man says, the war's long gone. I've got all the trouble I can handle, thinking of how I can drive those ornery sonsuv-bitches way across the Red and into Kansas with only half a regular crew.' Sam Ford turned and faced Frank. 'Mister,' he said, 'I don't give a damn about you being a blue belly. You can be General Sherman himself in disguise. All I want to know is can you work with cattle?'

'Not on this scale, Mr Ford,' Frank admitted, pointing to the herd. 'But I worked on my father's farm before I went off to fight in the war. I can work iron, mend fences, general stuff like that.'

Sam Ford pushed his hat back bearing a bald pate that glistened in the sun's rays. He spat on the small branding-iron fire in disgust. 'A Yankee sodbuster, that's all that I need.' He gave Frank a God-help-me look.

Frank looked at the battered tin cups half filled with coffee and the cold greasy bacon and beans congealed on the plates lying on the ground. He smiled at the Double Star foreman. 'M'be I don't know much about herding longhorns, Mr Ford,' he said. 'But I can sure fix better grub than the fella that dished up that swill.'

Sam Ford dropped the branding-iron to the ground as though he had got hold of the hot end. 'You can?' he almost yelled. 'You ain't just tryin' to fool an old cowhand?' The rest of the Double Star crew showed the same excited looks on their faces.

Frank's smile widened. 'I'll bet my horse and saddle on it, Mr Ford. My pa and ma ran an eating house back in the old country. They sold it up and came to America and bought themselves a farm. Just to keep their hands in they used to do all the catering for our neighbours' weddings and birthday dances. It was only natural as I was growing up I picked up a few points here and there. But that don't mean I'm as good in fixing grub as a chef in a fancy hotel.'

'My boys ain't fancy eaters, Mister er …?' said Sam Ford, looking quizzically at Frank.

'Eberhart, Frank Eberhart, Mister Ford,' Frank

said.

'Well, Frank,' continued the ranch foreman, 'as long as you can dish up beans that ain't burnt and coffee that don't taste like coal tar we'll be happy and won't want to nail your hide to a barn door for being a lowdown Yankee ploughboy.'

Frank grinned at the foreman. 'Then you've just hired yourself a cook, Mr Ford.'

Sam Ford returned his smile. 'No need for the title now that you're one of the crew, plain sonuvabitch will do, as long as I can't hear you.' He spoke to one of the ranch-hands. 'Ben, show the new cook where the bunkhouse is and give him a hand to see to his horse then take him along the cookhouse. Tell Waco he has to vacate the cookhouse, pronto. Tell him also that if he as much as opens a tin of beans, let alone tries to cook them, again, I'll shoot his ears off.'

TWO

The Double Star's newly-hired hand looked round the inside of the cookhouse and thought that he should have lied to Sam Ford; Told him that he'd played around with longhorns since before he was britched, knew all about their cantankerous ways. It would have been an easier chore riding the herd than cleaning up the mess he was gazing at to get the place reasonably clean so that he could cook food in it without the crew being poisoned.

Waco, a small, weasel-faced man, was bent low over a battered, rusty field cooker feeding logs into its firebox when he and Ben walked up to the cookhouse. After hearing about Sam's orders Waco straightened up and loosened the apron he had tied round his middle and handed it to Frank. Frank reckoned that the apron had once been white, now it was as black and stained as the cooker. And he had smelt sweeter smelling horse blankets. He could appreciate Sam Ford's desperation to find himself a cook. The crew must have a strong sense of loyalty to Mrs Farrow, and stronger stomachs to eat chow prepared by a dirty little runt like Waco. He wouldn't let the son-of-a-bitch feed hogs.

'About time Ford got himself a cook,' whined Waco. 'I was hired to tend cattle not to fix chow for

16

ungrateful bastards who beef about every morsel I put before them. Even though I've sweated my balls off doing it.' He eyed Frank with water-filled, smoke-reddened eyes. 'You'll find out, mister, that I speak the truth. They forget that they're only a bunch of dollar-a-day assholes. Yet they expect to sit down to their ma's home cookin'. Why if they'd been red nigras they would be eating boiled dog and likin' it.'

A straight-faced Ben said, 'Ain't that what we've been eatin', Waco? It sure tasted like dog. Only I reckon that an Injun cook would have boiled it more tender before he dished it out.'

Waco let loose a string of mule-skinner oaths and curses at him then walked away from the cooker in a pigeon-toed horse rider's roll.

'It's all yours, Yankee,' said Ben. 'The two night riders expect to eat at about six o'clock, before going out to relieve the day crew at the beef grazing on the south range. The rest of us, eight hands, reckon to sit down for chow at seven. 'He gave Frank a sympathetic better-you-than-me-pal grin. 'You've got your work cut out and that's a fact, Yankee. Me, I'd rather stick to chivvying longhorns around for my due.' He touched his hat in a mock salute and followed Waco's path to the herd and the branding. Frank stepped inside the cookhouse forewarned by the former cook's appearance and by what he'd seen and heard about the standard of Waco's culinary attempts knew that he wasn't about to enter into a shiny bright palace of a kitchen.

Frank sighed resignedly as he took off his coat and began rolling up his shirt sleeves. He had come here to help the widow Farrow and he reckoned

that the feeding of her crew would have to do for
starters so he would just have to knuckle down and
do it.

Several hours of scraping, scouring and scrub-
bing plus several gallons of hot water, and as much
sweat, transformed the cookhouse into a place that
even his pa would deem fit and proper to prepare
and cook food in. There were plenty of rations in
the cookhouse, a fresh side of beef, eggs, sowbelly,
beans and flour and potatoes. Mrs Farrow certainly
didn't intend starving her crew Frank thought. All
she lacked was a man with the skill and the
inclination to turn those dry rations into a meal
that was eatable.

When the two night riders came into the
cookhouse they were greeted with the savoury,
mouth-watering smell of slow frying steak and
onions, newly baked bread rolls and fresh brewed
coffee; and the sight of glistening sand polished
eating irons and tin plates laid out on a scrubbed
white eating-off table. Frank, wearing a clean
apron, eyed them both for their reactions. One of
them seemed hardly out of his teens and he could
understand Sam Ford's concern about the shortage
of experienced trail-hands for the coming drive
north.

'Well I'll be durned,' the younger one gasped.
'We've seen a miracle being worked, Chris, a
genuine miracle.' Both their still sleep-drawn faces
lit up.

Frank gave them a big welcoming grin. 'Just help
yourselves to some coffee, boys, then sit yourselves
down. Will steak, eggs and beans and potatoes suit
you, followed by fresh baked rolls and syrup?'

Both ranch-hands could only nod dumbly, still

taken aback by the transformation that had taken place in the cookhouse. The one that had spoken about miracles happening did the talking again. Voice soft, full of the awe and amazement he was still feeling, he murmured, 'Has one of the boys finally put a Winchester shell through that asshole Waco's dirty hide, mister?'

'Mr Ford threatened to do just that if Waco attempted to put on the cook's apron again,' answered Frank. 'I'm Frank Eberhart, the new cook.'

'I'm Charlie,' the talkative ranch-hand said. 'This here is my buddy, Chris. If your grub tastes as good as it smells, Frank, then you've got two friends for life, for the pair of us won't be night ridin' the herd with unsettled guts. Waco's hash used to screw them up something cruel. Ain't that the truth, Chris?'

'It sure is, Charlie,' replied Chris. 'How that little weasel-faced sonuvabitch lived so long as a cook is a mystery.' He grinned expectantly at Frank. 'We're ready when you are, Mr Eberhart.' He picked up his knife and fork. 'Just you heap it on our plates; we're growin' boys and we've a long cold night ahead of us.'

Frank watched them leave the cookhouse with a feeling of deep satisfaction. Not because they had enjoyed his cooking, and told him so, but neither of them had made any remarks about him being a Yankee. Frank grinned to himself. It looked as though he had to win the acceptance and respect of the ranch crew through pandering to their bellies. The real test would come when the full crew came in for their chow. Frank wiped the table down then began cutting off steaks from the side of beef in readiness for their appearance but he was interrupted in his task by the entry into the cookhouse of a young boy, that Frank knew could only be Lee Farrow, the junior boss man of the Double Star. He didn't hesitate in asking about his new cook's background.

'Is it true, Mr Eberhart, that you were a blue-belly?' he said. 'Mr Ford told me you were.'

Frank stopped what he was doing and looked down at the earnest-faced boy. He could detect no sign of hostility at his facing a man who once wore the hated uniform of the soldiers that killed his pa, just boyish curiosity. Would he still look at him in the same innocent way Frank wondered when the boy found out that he was responsible for the death of his pa?

'Yeah it's true, boy,' he said. 'I once wore the blue of the Union. At the time it seemed the right thing to do. After all I am a Yankee.'

'Yankee blue-bellies killed my pa, Mr Eberhart,' Lee said. Frank saw the slight trembling of the boy's lower lip and the child's face began to show through his manly stoic mask.

'Did they now?' replied Frank soberly. 'I also know lots of Union boys whose pas were killed by Johnny Rebs. By the way, boy, I see that you know my name.' Frank smiled. 'But I'm not acquainted with yours,' he lyingly said.

'Oh, I'm Lee Farrow. Owner of the Double Star. Or I will be in eight years time when I'm eighteen, so Mom says.'

'Now what about you and me, boss, sitting down at the table and over coffee and a fresh bread roll and syrup you can tell me all about the ornery habits of the longhorns you own. Mr Ford told me

I must get to know all their stubborn ways if I want to go on the drive to Kansas with the rest of the crew. If I don't he'll boot me off your ranch. You see, Lee, I was a sodbuster in Minnesota before I came south to seek out my kin. You being a cattleman will know the joshin' I'll get off the boys when they find out I was just a poor dirt-farmer. Why I hear that in Texas a sodbuster is lower than a sheep herder in the run of things.'

Lee solemnly shook his head. 'Not lower, Mr Eberhart, just about the same level.' Face brightening up he said, 'Now tell me what you want to know about ranch work.'

'Gladly, Lee,' replied Frank. 'But why don't we start on those rolls and syrup as we jaw. I've a feeling that hearing about all the hard work that goes on here at the Double Star will raise in me one heck of an appetite, OK?'

'I can see that there's been a lot of hard work in here in this cookhouse, Mr Eberhart.'

Frank paused in his preparation of the roll, the knife, motionless in mid-air, dripping molasses from its blade. He looked at Mrs Farrow standing in the doorway.

'I wouldn't say no to a cup of your coffee, Mr Eberhart,' Mrs Farrow said. 'It smells delicious and after a ride from Sweet Springs a drink would go down well.' She smiled. 'I'm Mrs Farrow, the owner of the Double Star. I see that you have already met my son. Sam Ford has just told me that he'd hired a new cook.'

Frank ignored the mess the molasses was making on his clean table. He was too occupied with taking in the slender-figured widow. Mrs Farrow was a lot thinner in the face than her photo in the watchcase.

Lines breaking the smoothness of her skin about
the eyes, streaks of grey showing in the blue-black
hair. Not all to do with ageing as Frank well knew.
She hardly seemed as old as he was yet Captain
Farrow had looked as though he was in his late
forties. He thought that if she had been his wife he
would have let a whole company of the enemy roast
rather than risk his neck any more than he had to
in a war. Keeping himself alive for her would have
always been the top priority. Captain Farrow had
been one hell of a man. Somehow he felt, when he
did eventually get round to telling her the reason
for his coming to the Double Star, she would show
the same sympathy and compassion her husband
definitely had. Frank ceased ruminating on what
may or may not happen at sometime in the future.
He had a job to hold down.

'Young Lee and me were just settling down for a
quiet chat,' he said.

Mrs Farrow looked closely at her son. 'You
haven't been annoying Mr Eberhart, Lee, have
you? He has a lot of work to do you know.'

'No, Mom,' answered Lee. 'I was just about to tell
Mr Eberhart how we do things on the ranch. He's a
Yankee sodbuster, Mom.'

Mrs Farrow turned sharply on her son. 'There
are no Yankees here, boy,' she angrily snapped.
'Only ranch-hands, understand?' Then just as
quickly her voice softened to normal as she added,
'Your father would have wanted it so; the hatred
between us and the North ended when the war
ended.'

Captain Farrow's widow was an equally fine
person thought Frank as he placed the tray with
the coffee and rolls on the table. He waited till Mrs

Farrow had sat down alongside her boy before he took a seat opposite them. Mrs Farrow took a sip at her coffee.

'It's good,' she said.

Frank beamed at her from across the table. 'Waco's apology for coffee didn't need much beating, Mrs Farrow.'

Mrs Farrow smiled and the worry lines on her face vanished for a moment.

'I offered to clean up this place, Mr Eberhart,' she said. 'But Sam wouldn't hear of it. Said it was the ranch-hands business to see to their own cooking arrangements. If they wanted to eat like hogs so be it. It wasn't for me to mollycoddle them. I told him that a crew must be well fed or we'll lose them. Sam told me not to worry, things would sort themselves out. I think that he's pinning his hopes on you, Mr Eberhart.' This time her smile was more natural, easier coming. 'By what I've seen of what you have done so far I think that he has chosen wisely.'

Frank blushed at the compliment. 'As I said, ma'am, Waco couldn't boil water without burning it. And there's no reason for any man that professes to call himself a cook to dish up lousy chow, beggin' your pardon, ma'am. There's plenty of rations to go at. Enough to provide good meals for a crew twice as big.'

'I suppose there isn't, Mr Eberhart,' replied Mrs Farrow. 'But most of the crew are mere boys. No more than six or seven years older than Lee. The rest are old men, good ranch-hands I know, but more at home on a horse or in a saloon than doing a cook's work.' Mrs Farrow gave Frank a long, and to him, a pleading look before saying, 'I hope you will stay, Mr Eberhart.'

Frank grinned at her. 'If the crew can stand an ex-blue-belly fixing their chow, ma'am, then I'll stay.'

Mrs Farrow got to her feet. 'I think that it is time we were going Lee, we must not stop Mr Eberhart from getting on with his work. Thanks for the coffee and rolls.' She smiled. 'I think the boys are in for a treat tonight by what I can smell of your cooking.'

'Can I stay a while, Mom, please?' Lee said. 'Mr Eberhart and me haven't had our talk yet.'

Mrs Farrow cast a questioning glance at Frank. A ghost of a smile crossed his face as he gave a slight nod of his head.

'OK, Lee, you can stay,' Mrs Farrow said. 'But only if you promise not to get in Mr Eberhart's way. And don't forget you've got some book learning to do before you go to bed so don't stay too long, understand?'

'Thanks, Mom,' said Lee. 'I won't be a nuisance, I promise.' He swung round on his chair to face Frank. 'Now, Mr Eberhart, what exactly do you want me to tell you about work on a cattle ranch.'

It was a tired but well satisfied Frank that made his way to the bunkhouse on the outcome of his first day at the ranch. He had been a little apprehensive when the rest of the crew had come in for the evening meal. There could have been several more of them with the same feelings as the crippled boy, Phil, that it was still open season for the shooting down of Yankees. But everything had gone off peaceful-like, apart from the occasional fierce scowl from Phil. Frank put it down to the meal of grilled steaks, eggs and beans, second helpings if wanted, that the boys tore into to like a pack of starving wolves, and he didn't doubt, Sam Ford, for putting out the hard word, hands off the new Yankee cook or you'll be sitting down eating Waco's pig swill again.

Sam Ford, sitting on the edge of his bunk drawing at his pipe, nodded to Frank as he walked in. He took the pipe out of his mouth and swept it round the room in a pointing gesture. 'The sonsuvbitches are sleeping like little babies, Frank. Hear them snoring their heads off? There's nothing like a good hot meal, or a good hot woman to make a man sleep as though he was never goin' to wake up again. I did positively hire you, Yankee, didn't I?' he growled good naturedly. 'Tophand's wages I recollect.'

'You sure did, boss,' replied Frank and sitting down on his own bunk began removing his boots. He had won the Double Star crew's bellies, how long was it going to take before he won their trust and friendship? How long would it be before they did not see him as a former enemy? Only time would tell. Yet he had a good feeling that he could help Mrs Farrow in the running of her ranch, enough to pay off his debt to Mr Farrow and satisfy his conscience. That thought let him fall alseep as soon as his head hit the pillow.

Mrs Farrow was having more than a few thoughts of her own to ruminate over before she settled down for the night. Through Lee's excitingly told account of his conversation with Mr Eberhart before he finally dropped off to sleep she now knew more about the background of the ranch's new cook than the brief history Sam had told her about his new hiring. She wondered why Mr Eberhart had travelled all the way from

Minnesota just to take a cook's job on a small ranch when his obvious talent for cooking could have easily got him a job with more pay with one of the bigger ranches.

And why had he not stayed on his father's farm? He was a hard worker, and what little time she had spent with him she assessed him as being strong-willed, yet not a blowhard. A man with hidden strength he would only let surface when absolutely necessary. A man with a character not unlike her late husband's. Isobel put his wandering down to the after effects of the war. What else would make a man capable of running his own farm leave his roots to come as far south as this? Men not only came out of the war with visible wounds and scars but with minds unsettled by the horrors they had been through. Whatever reason had brought Mr Eberhart to the Double Star, his showing up had solved a problem that had been plaguing her and Sam Ford for weeks. She was confident now that when the Double Star cattle set off for the long trail to Abilene whatever else the crew would have to face, hostile Indians, floods, drought, they would at least not go hungry.

Suddenly, for no apparent reason, Mrs Farrow began to compare the new cook with her husband; their physical similarities, both tall men, with strong-boned faces; capable of bold-facing any man or problem, yet gentle enough to win the confidence and trust of children. Mr Eberhart had proved that. Lee, back there in the cookhouse, had forgotten for a while the father he would never see again. Yes, she thought, they were very much akin in all ways. She wondered if Mr Eberhart was married and had a family. Mrs Farrow smiled. Lee on being told that the new cook's father and mother were German had asked her how it was that a German could be a Yankee blue-belly.

Mrs Farrow's felt the tears run warm and salty down her cheeks. Thinking about Mr Eberhart had let loose emotions and fears that she had struggled to hold back for Lee's sake. Several times since she had heard the dreadful news of James being killed in battle she felt that she hadn't the strength of purpose or the will to hold on to the ranch. Indeed if it hadn't been for Sam telling her that she had to hang on in for Lee's sake, as that would be what the Captain would expect her to do, she would have sold the place and gone south to her folk. Now that she was almost ready to send the ranch's first herd north those earlier fears of not being able to cope were returning. How could a widow, raising a boy, be expected to run a ranch she bitterly thought. Dear God how she missed James.

It had been in the fall of '55, when James had taken over the ownership of a holding that had been left to him by an uncle who had recently died. It was, James said, to be their dream ranch and had asked her to name it. She had – the Double Star. A lucky star for each of them. They saw it for the first time coming down the Brazos river trail. Newly-weds, with all they possessed wrapped up in tarp bundles and crates in the back of the big plains wagon James was driving.

The outbuildings were in need of repair but the large double-storeyed stone and timber built house, though paint-flaked, looked structurally sound. They had been told that there was stock on the land, how many and what, horses or cattle, they didn't know yet, and that there was a Mexican family acting as caretakers of the holding till the new owners arrived.

James Farrow pulled hard at the reins of the four-horse team dragging them to a hoof-kicking dust halt on the rim of the basin. He smiled at his young wife.

'It doesn't look much, Isobel,' he said. 'But it's all ours, not a leasehold held by some grasping fingered banker in Fort Worth. There's water and lots of good grass. Enough to be able to feed a sizeable herd. And the house looks fine enough as it is; with a lick of paint here and there and the odd window shutter renewing, it will make a grand big house worthy of the Double Star cattle ranch. I know it isn't as big as your father's ranch, Isobel, we haven't got the land he's got and we are only starting out but between us we'll make something of it that we'll both be proud to hand down to our family. When we begin raising one,' he added, grinning widely.

Isobel laughed and squeezed her husband's hand reassuringly. 'You should have seen my father's place when I was a young girl. So don't worry, James, we'll build that home we have always dreamed about. As you say, it is all ours. What spare cash we can raise won't have to be handed over to the bankers. We can use it to build up the herd.' Isobel reached up and kissed her husband. Bold-smiling him she said, 'M'be spend some of the money getting a room fixed up in the house for the first of the family you intend raising.'

Isobel remembered that she wasn't really all that interested in the grass or the water and the size of the herd that one day would graze on Double Star land. All she saw was how grand the house would look when it was cleaned up and freshly painted. The colour of the drapes she would hang at the windows, the patterns on the carpets, the big, deep-seated wine-coloured hide chairs. A place a woman would feel comfortable in when she gave birth to her first child – news she had not told James. She had just sat silent beside him on the wagon seat holding his hand, feeling the excitement flowing through him as he savoured the mental pictures of the ranch as it would be, God willing, one day. That had been his moment. Hers would come later when she told him that she was with child.

God had proved himself willing and slowly they built up the ranch. The first winter had been a blessedly mild one and James had lost none of his first-year calves. The ranch boasted two hired hands on the payroll. Young boys, Phil and Chris, but good cattlemen, a great help to James who had thinned down considerably with the long hard hours he put in. The house had been furnished to her taste and baby Lee was coming up to his first birthday. She had been all set to suggest to James that Lee should have a brother or a sister to grow up with when a Texas Ranger had ridden up with the fearful news that a hostile warband was out raiding and burning in the territory.

She couldn't rightly recollect the Indian chief's name but she knew that it was a band of Kiowas that were doing the killing. The ranger seeing that the house was mainly stone built said that they should stay close to it, fort-up in it if things came to the worst. It could mean that they could lose some of their stock and barns being burnt down but as the ranger bluntly put it to them that was better than losing one's hair. All of James' grand plans for the ranch had to hang fire. Staying alive was all that mattered.

Every day they watched anxiously from the look-out post for the ominous signs of dust clouds closing in on the ranch. They had to sleep in rotation, always two on guard, loaded weapons by their sides. Only later was she told that James had wrung a promise out of the two boys that if he got killed they had to make certain that she and Lee didn't get taken alive by the Kiowa. Isobel felt as though cold hands had been laid on her bare flesh. The years hadn't washed away the pure terror she had lived with in those black days. But God had not completely forgotten them. He sent them Sam Ford. Without his timely help her and James' dream for the future would have been for naught. They would have all been dead, massacred by the Kiowas.

Chris acting as look-out yelled, 'Single rider comin' in, Mr Farrow.'

James Farrow lowered his Winchester and felt the tightness at his chest ease a little. He held a hand, palm down, across his brow to shield his eyes from the fierce glare of the high-noon-sun's rays. When the rider rode clear of the heat haze James could see that he was a short, broad-built man. Dust-shrouded, strained-faced, the look of a man that had done a lot of hard riding.

'Welcome to the Double Star ranch, sir,' James said. 'There's water for your horse at the back of the barn there and coffee brewing if you care to step down. I'm James Farrow, owner of the Double Star. That's my good lady wife with our son standing on the porch. These two boys are my crew.'

'Thanks, Mr Farrow,' Sam Ford said. 'A cup of coffee would be mighty welcome.' He pushed the rifle he had been holding across his saddle horn back into its boot then dismounted. He raised his hat to Mrs Farrow with a curt, "Ma'am." When he saw her go inside the house for what he assumed was to see to the coffee he said, 'Do you know about the Indians being out causing trouble, Mr Farrow? I didn't want to mention it in front of your good lady. By the way my name is Sam Ford.' He grinned at James. 'From no particular location.'

'We know about the Indian trouble, Mr Ford,' replied James. 'And thanks for considering my wife's feelings, but she already knows.'

'The red devils are not too far away, Mr Farrow,' said Sam Ford. 'I cut fresh sign of a warband of at least eight or nine bucks fifteen miles west of here. There's a full moon tonight, a Kiowa moon. That means the wild boys won't be goin' to bed early tonight. There'll be plenty of light for them to carry on with their killin'." Sam Ford gave the ranch-house a quick but all-seeing look. 'Though I reckon a strong-built place like your home, Mr Farrow, will make them wait till the moon goes down and try to sneak up on you while it's dark. They're not lookin' for a fight, they're just out for a bit of killin' and suchlike Kiowa sport.'

'Thanks for your warning, Mr Ford,' said a grim-faced James. 'We are keeping a good look-out. By what you've told me we can't relax our guard one little bit if we are to stand a chance of driving them off if they do decide to attack us. What are your intentions, Mr Ford?'

Sam's intentions had been quite simple. As soon as his horse had been fed and watered and he had obliged the good lady of the house by drinking her coffee he would say his farewells and ass-kick it eastwards to put as much ground between him and the Indian sign he had discovered before that great big, bright as daylight, Kiowa moon came up. That was till he saw Mrs Farrow with the baby in her arms standing there on the porch, all white-faced and scared looking. He knew exactly what would be going through Mr Farrow's mind. The same fear, but not showing it for his wife's sake, a touch of panic and helplessness, cursing himself for bringing his wife, and now his son, into this hellhole of a land just to get them both butchered.

A long time ago he had asked himself the same question looking at the smouldering ruins of his home, five years of blood and sweat turned into a blackened heap. He never did find his wife or his boy and he searched for over a year. He then drifted across into New Mexico, below the Rio Grande and back into Texas, working on cattle spreads till the pain had gone. Sam could see by the jut of Mr Farrow's jaw he wasn't about to let his fears soften his determination to make a stand, fight to protect his family and home. By the look of the two young ranch-hands' faces they were willing to earn more than their pay by staying to back up their boss in protecting the ranch. Sam made up his mind. He had been unable to save his own family but by hell he would give Mr Farrow what help he was capable of so that his pretty young wife and her baby didn't meet the same fate his wife and boy had.

'I'll stay, Mr Farrow,' he said. 'Give you an extra gun if needs be.'

'We'll be glad of your assistance, Mr Ford,' James said. 'Heartfelt glad. But I don't wish to delay you on your journey or ask you to share our danger.'

Sam smiled. 'I ain't headin' for any place special. And as for sharing your danger, Mr Farrow, it could be a durn sight more dangerous for me wandering out there on my ownsome. Could get jumped by the sonsuvbitches at any time. Four of us here could put up a rare old fight, m'be scare them off if they do come this far. Now why don't I see to my horse, then we'll go inside and have that coffee and discuss tactics.'

They had come at night, when the moon was low and partially blanketed by clouds, as Sam had predicted. Again thanks to Sam, James and the boys were ready for them. She had been upstairs in the main bedroom with Lee wrapped up in a blanket in her arms. A fully-loaded pistol lay on a nearby table. She had known she could never use it to put an end to Lee's life and her own even if the red devils burst into the room. She had been so brain-numbed with fear that she had only a vague recollection of the short but bloody events of that night.

The bird calls came first, then she thought she could see slow moving shadowy figures down by the big feed barn. The roar and flash of pistols, fired by Sam and one of the boys lying in ambush behind the smithy wall, lit up the darkness and broke the silence of the night, proving that what she had seen were not merely figments of her highly-charged nervous state of mind. James and Phil, the other ranch-hand, joined in the firing from a ground floor window. In ten minutes it was all over and quietness came over the ranch again. And it became praying time for her till first light.

Pistols and rifles held at the ready the four men had come warily out of the house and the smithy. They told her later that they had counted five dead Kiowas; she was told to stay inside the house till they had been decently buried. The threat to their well-being was over. Her resolve not to kill Lee and herself hadn't been put to the ultimate test and she thanked God for that.

Sam was hired as ranch foreman and piece by bitter piece she and James got to know about his past life and realized that Sam had taken on more than the ranch foreman's job. He had taken on the responsibility of watching over the Farrow family, looking out for them like a favourite uncle. They were making up for the emptiness in his life Sam had suffered by losing his own family.

His quiet, comforting strength had prevented her from cracking up when the terrible news of James' death was broken to her. Now she was a real boss lady, respected by her crew and the other ranchers, and almost ready to drive her first herd north to the stockyards at Abilene. She had not let James down. Lee would take over a fine ranch when he came of age. Isobel dabbed her eyes and cheeks dry and lay back on her pillow. Her last thought, puzzling her till she finally fell asleep, was that even in the short time she had known him she sensed that Mr Eberhart had the same inner strength to give to her and the Double Star that Sam Ford had. Or maybe she was just imagining it all. But why had she began comparing him to her husband, evoking all those past bitter sweet memories? Isobel sighed deeply and pulled the sheets over her shoulders and called it a day. A boss lady had more important, real practical things to ponder over, like running a ranch and bringing up a boy, than lie awake half the night fantasizing about the inner feelings of the ranch cook.

THREE

The men squatting round the small smokeless fire in a brush-hidden hollow some fifteen miles north of the Red River deep in Indian territory were an unshaven bunch of hard-faced looking men, taking men, garbed in a mixture of gear; some in well-worn homespuns, a few favouring Union army tunics matched with store pants, others dressed in blue-belly yellow striped cavalry pants with civilian jackets, two with what they wore covered by dirty linen dusters. Only the man with captain's bars pinned to his army tunic was garbed in the full uniform of a Union officer. Captain Milton Hardin also wore thigh length red leather boots as befitting a former member of Colonel Lane's "Red Leg" anti-slavery guerrillas that had upheld the Union cause in the Kansas-Missouri border country before and during the war. What they all had in common was the prices on their heads, dead or alive – double for Captain Hardin's scalp – for crimes of murder and robbery against civilians, reb and unionist, carried out in the name of the Union.

The Kansas "Red Legs" had fought for the Union against their southern counterparts, "Bloody" Bill Anderson's raiders and William

Quantrill's guerrillas. The battles the irregulars fought lost sight of the main principles of the Civil War; it was the time for settling old scores and grievances in the border country. They didn't believe in such hogwash as being chivalrous and gentlemanly in the pursuing of their cause, such as allowing their enemy to surrender, treating his wounded or praising his gallantry. They fought under the black flag of no quarter given, or sought. Their hallmark was merciless dead-of-night raids that left women and children, old folk, lying dead in the flames of their burning homes.

Even before the war had ended such bands were disowned by the governments they fought for, outcasts wanted by both sides in the conflict, some of them like Captain Milton Hardin, not accepting the South's surrender. Once a reb always a reb. No piece of paper signed by the biggest traitor of them all, General Robert E Lee, would convince him otherwise. There had been too much blood spilt for such Christian charitable acts as forgiveness. Old hatreds die hard. None more so than in "bleeding" Kansas and her "dark and bloody ground."

To Captain Hardin, stealing Texas cattle was one way of keeping his war going and the means of feeding and clothing his men. He also saw to their recreation – having enough cash to partake in the pleasures that the spangle-dressed women of the bawdy houses offered in Abilene and the regular supply of hard men's drinking liquor.

A rider pushed his way through the brush and came down into the hollow. The small talk ceased and the men eyed each other expectantly across the fire, ready for when the captain said jump. Men who rode with Captain Hardin slept on their bellies, one eye open, fast reaction men. They had to be to stay alive. It was a sneaky, hit and run Indian-type war, no beating drums or blaring bugles, that had been fought in the woods and brush along the Kansas-Missouri line.

Sergeant Kegg, Captain Hardin's second-in-command, got to his feet and walked over to the captain to hear the report that Tod would be making. Clem Tod, a small but burly big-bellied man, dismounted and saluted Captain Hardin.

'The herd's bedded down for the night, Capt'n,' he said. 'Only two night riders nursing them. The rest of the crew, no more than eight or nine hands, are bedded down at the cook's wagon in a grab of timber about half a mile south of the beef.' Tod gave a gap-toothed grin. 'Should be no problem cutting out a sizeable chunk of the herd, Capt'n.'

Captain Hardin's long ploughshare-angled face softened slightly in a smile that had as much humour in it as Clem Tod's grin. 'Good work, Tod,' he said. 'Grab yourself a bite to eat and some coffee.' The captain turned and faced Sergeant Kegg. 'We'll hit 'em an hour after the moon comes up, Sergeant. By then the secessionist sonsuv-bitches should be fast asleep dreaming of the delights their pay will buy them in Abilene. Prepare the men to be ready to move out in an hour.'

Sergeant Kegg gave a barked, 'Sir!' in response to the captain's orders and turned on his heels and strode back to the men at the camp fire. 'OK boys,' he said. 'It's coming up to party time. See to your weapons and horses, we move out in an hour.'

The raiders rein-led their horses till not only

could they smell the presence of the herd but saw its dark undulating mass silhouetted in the brilliant moonlight. No spoken words of command were given. They had all been briefed back at the hollow so every man knew what was expected of him. Besides, night raiding came as natural as eating, drinking and going to the crapper. Tod, in spite of the fat he was carrying, could move as silent as a marauding hostile buck. He was also as expert with the use of a knife as an Indian. He was to see to it that the two night men were despatched with the minimum of fuss and noise.

Six men under Sergeant Kegg's command were detailed to lift the cattle, as many longhorns as they could push along fast, and scatter the rest to the far corners of the nation. The remainder of the raiders with Captain Hardin at their head would ride down on the trail-drivers' camp after Tod had given the OK signal. There they would shoot at the sleeping blanket-wrapped men, set fire to the cook's wagon and generally stomp into the dirt anyone that put up a fight. If there were any men fit and bold enough to get astride a horse after they had stormed through they would be too busy trying to round up the spooked part of the herd to trail an unknown number of cattle lifters across unfamiliar territory at night.

The left-hand loop rider was blessing someone he had read about in the papers back at the ranch in Texas. A Mr J McCoy. That easterner had made a deal with the railroad cmpany to run a line westards, to Abilene, Kansas. That meant instead of a long haul westwards to the cattle pens at the trail's end town of Sedalia. Missouri, the herd could be pointed due north on an easy trail that led

across the North Canadian, the Cimarron then into
Kansas and the welcoming fleshpots of Abilene.
The rider grinned. Reckoning that what they could
offer was only fair recompense for men that had
hard-assed it the full length of the Chisholm Trail
chivvying a herd of longhorns along for a dollar a
day and all found. The trail-hand suddenly felt
himself being yanked out of his saddle. 'What the
hell!' he gasped out, thinking that it was one of the
boys horsing around.

Something cold ran a nerve-tingling line across
his throat, then came a sticky warmness that
flooded down his neck, his life's blood. Tod
lowered a dead man to the ground. The horse
snorted in fear and kicked dirt up with its feet as it
smelt the fresh blood. Tod patted it soothingly on
the neck till it calmed down. He put the dead man's
broad-brimmed plain hat and long outer coat on
and mounted his own horse. He rode the circuit of
the herd till he met the right-hand loop man.

'Next time round, Jim,' the rider called out to
Tod as he came nearer. 'I'll swing back to the camp
and get us some coffee before my balls drop off. I'll
need them for sure when we hit Abilene. Hey ...
you ain't Jim!' Before he could ask Tod what the
hell he was doing here Tod acted. His right hand
flicked sharply outwards. The moon's rays reflected on the knife's blade on its brief but deadly
winging flight. Tod heard the dull thuck of the
knife striking home and the man's pain-rasped
gasp and watched him fold at the middle and fall
across his horse's neck like a burst feed sack.

He kneed his horse closer and lifted up the dead
man and pulled out his knife from his chest, wiped
it on the shirt before letting the body drop back on

to the saddle, then slipped it back into the sheath
that hung by a cord around his neck. Cupping his
hands to his mouth Tod gave the all clear signal.
The waiting raiders heard the plaintive cry of a
hunting night bird. It was time for the captain's
party to make its move. Leaving Sergeant Kegg
and his men waiting for Tod's return and the next
signal, more blood-racing than a night owl's call,
the sound of pistol discharges and the screams and
shouts of men being gunned down.

The raiders moved in on the trail-herders' camp
slowly, line abreast so that when the firing started
no raider would fall foul of a bullet fired by his own
kind. A slight movement in the brush in front of
him caught Captain Hardin's eyes. He raised a
white-gloved hand, the line of riders halted. A man
stepped into view, buttoning up his flies. He lifted
his head and in the full moon's light he clearly saw
the horsemen with pistols fisted ready for use.

'Jesus Christ!' he mouthed in alarm and brought
up the Winchester he held under his right arm.
Captain Hardin stretched out his pistol arm across
his horse's neck and pulled off a load. The
long-barrelled cap and ball Walker bucked and
flamed in his hand. Its heavy slug tore away most
of the trail-hand's face in a bloody welter of flesh
and bone. The small massacre had begun. Men,
half dressed, half asleep, rolled out of their
blankets in panic, grabbing for rifles or pistols only
to be cut down by the hail of lead aimed at them by
the yelling, whooping raiders pounding over their
camp site.

Sergeant Kegg and his detail heard the firing
and the yelling, saw the flames of the cook's wagon
reaching above the tree tops. He wolf-grinned at

his men. 'OK, boys, let's go and get the Capt'n his quota of beef. Slim and Jake, you hang back a piece just in case any of the sonsuvbitches come high-tailin' it up from the camp.' His grin broadened, became almost human. 'Though by the sound of way things seemed to be goin' I reckon that's mighty unlikely.'

FOUR

Frank had only been at the ranch three days when along with Phil he made the regular wagon trip into Sweet Springs to pick up supplies. Phil insisted that he held the reins and did the driving. Frank reckoned that it was to prove to the asshole he was sitting beside that a one-armed Johnny Reb could still hold down a man's job. Phil, although he ate the food with the rest of the them, still had the big hate for former blue-bellies. Frank could sympathize part of the way with his thinking; it was a lot for a young kid to lose, an arm and an eye. And if it had been him that had suffered the injuries he would have no doubt felt some bitterness against the rebs in general but the war had ended and so had the hatred. General Lee had known that and so damnit Phil had to get the message also.

Phil drew up the wagon close against the loading bay of the only general merchandise store that Frank could see fronting Main Street, Sweet Springs, next to what seemed the only drinking establishment in the town. Frank thought that m'be he could get Phil to go in for a beer after they had loaded the wagon. Possibly get the kid to unbend a little, be more sociable towards him. Not that Frank had any high hopes of a glass of beer changing

Phil's opinion of him if he did take up his offer, but
at least it showed that he was willing to meet the kid
more than halfway to try and make friends with
him. All he had got from the kid on the ride from
the ranch was a series of grunts in answer to
anything he asked him. But the former blue-belly
was to win the friendship of Phil sooner than he
anticipated.

They both stepped down from the wagon and
Phil pointed to a pile of crates and packages by the
side of the store door. 'Them's ours, Yankee,' he
growled, and grabbed hold of the heaviest looking
crate and began dragging it to the wagon,
red-faced and panting with the effort. Frank
ground his teeth in frustrated anger. One arm or
not he felt like punching some sense in the kid.
Instead he roughly pushed Phil aside and grabbing
hold of the crate with both hands, heaved it up on
to the wagon. Phil turned on him, face working in
anger and Frank was set to have a showdown with
him; he'd about had his belly full of his sourness
towards him.

The noise of voices raised in drunken bonhomie
put an abrupt end to their confrontation for the
moment. They both turned and saw three men
come staggering out of the saloon, helping each
other along as they progressed towards them,
stopping just short of the pile of supplies. One of
them, a man as big as Frank, but running to fat
across his middle, whispered something to his
compadres that set them all laughing. He looked at
Frank and Phil with whiskey-clouded eyes.

'I was just sayin' to my pals, here, Phil,' he said,
'that I was wondering who the next in line was to
jump into bed with that purty widow woman that

bosses over you. I reckon it's that big fella with you. The cripples and old goats that the ranch has on its payroll don't stand a chance while he's around.'

Frank spun round the wagon, face hard-set in anger, and punched the ranch-hand, wrist deep, in his belly fat. The man's sneering face crumpled up into a broken agonized mask as he doubled up gasping for air. Frank's left cross, with all his weight behind it, caught the big-bellied man on the side of the jaw, a blow that felled him to the boardwalk like a pole-axed steer. One of the other men aimed a wild blow at Frank. Frank saw it coming and ducked and the man's fist passed harmlessly over his left shoulder. He pivoted on his right foot then brought up his left leg and kicked the ranch-hand in the crotch. Bar-room rules for bar-room hangers-on Frank fleetingly thought. The dirty-minded sons-of-bitches didn't deserve any break.

Phil involuntarily winced at the sound of the ranch-hand's high-pitched womanly scream of pain, then quickly stepped aside as the greenish-faced man threw up as he slowly sank to the boards cradling his balls. The third man sobering up fast, cursed and reached for the pistol at his right hip. Frank tried frantically to grab at the man's arm but the two inert bodies at his feet got in his way and he knew that he would be too late by a lifetime – his – to prevent the pistol from clearing leather and gunning him down.

A pistol cracked behind him and the ranch-hand yelped like a kicked dog, dropping his gun to the boards as with hurt-looking eyes he watched the blood running down his right hand. Frank twisted round and saw Phil with a still-smoking gun in his

fist. He nodded his thanks to him. Phil grinned
back. Men came spilling out of the saloon to see
what the shooting was about. A small-built man
with a big man's hard-eyed face gave Frank and
Phil an angry glare.

'What the hell's goin' on here?' he barked. 'Three
of my crew laid out!'

'They were dirty-mouthing Mrs Farrow, Mr
Craig,' Phil answered. 'My campadre here, Mr
Eberhart, our cook, took offence and knocked
those two boys of yours down. I winged the other
fella, Mr Craig, because he pulled a gun on Mr
Eberhart and he ain't totin' one. I was just aimin' to
keep the fight fair.'

Rancher Craig gave Frank a long scrutiny before
glancing down at his two ranch-hands. He looked
again at Phil. 'Cook did you say, boy? More like a
curly wolf to me.' He raised his voice. 'OK, OK, the
show's over. Some of you boys get these drunken
bums on to their horses and take them back to the
ranch to sleep it off. They only got what they
deserved. M'be they'll mind their manners in the
future.'

Phil had been doing some assessing of his own
from the moment he saw the big Yankee swing into
action. Frank had risked getting himself hurt real
bad – dead, if he hadn't pulled out his own gun –
tackling odds of three to one to protect the good
name of the boss, a woman the Yankee hardly
knew. Some blue-bellies Phil thought weren't so
bad after all. 'Let's get the wagon loaded, Yankee,'
he said, with all the former malice gone, 'then we
can go and have a beer before we head back to the
ranch. Seeing you in action has raised a thirst in
me.'

Frank gave a wide, open smile. 'I was about to make the same suggestion myself, reb, only I didn't think that you were old enough to partake.'

Over his beer Frank got to thinking of just why he had retaliated so quick and viciously against the ranch-hands. Coarse humour, dirty-mouthing had been the normal talk of the day in his spell in the army. And Mrs Farrow was only his boss and he had come to Texas to help her out not to get emotionally involved with her. Yet he acted as though she was close kin or he had some sort of claim on her. Frank opined that the beer he was drinking must be stronger than he reckoned for him to be thinking such fanciful thoughts. Yet Mrs Farrow must have got to him somehow; two men knocked cold in real anger proved that. Of course when he did get round to telling her how her husband met his death that feeling or whatever he thought he had about Mrs Farrow could be cut off short by Mrs Farrow herself by telling him to get the hell off the ranch. Frank cast a look at Phil. And the kid thought that he had problems he told himself; but they couldn't be as mixed up as his thinking right now.

FIVE

The crew were finishing off their evening meal and Frank was cleaning out his pans when Sam Ford and Mrs Farrow came into the cookhouse.

'Gather round, boys,' Sam said. 'The boss has some news she reckons you oughta know before we start the drive.'

Grave-faced, Mrs Farrow said, 'There's talk in Sweet Springs of most of the crew of the Lady Y from Sonora way being killed and their cattle stolen by raiders north of the Red River. The general opinion in the town is that the raiders were Kansas "Red Legs" led by a Captain Hardin.' Mrs Farrow smiled wanly. 'Sam said that I should not have told you about the killings. He said that trouble comes with the dollar a day and all found. I disagreed. All of you have helped to build up the ranch and I thank you for that loyalty. But loyalty doesn't mean that you have to give your lives for the Double Star so if any man wants what is owing to him so that he can move on, speak out. I'll understand.'

Frank watched, impassive-faced, for the crew's response. Again he was getting that close, warm feeling towards Mrs Farrow knowing that it was

48

make or break time for her. All his noble, good intentions were daydreams if the Double Star folded up. He could only hope and pray that the crew would stand by their boss.

It was Waco that voiced his opinion first. That surprised Frank till he reflected that Waco might be foul-mouthed, taciturn, not giving to bathing regularly, but he was also a tough, stubborn-minded Texan, hard bitten as a longhorn; a breed of man that would have to be hammered into the ground before he would admit defeat, as he damned well knew. He'd fought against the ornery, mule-headed sonsuvbitches at Chickamaugo.

Shuffling his feet like an embarrassed schoolboy Waco said, 'Yuh hired me tuh take the herd tuh Abilene, boss, and no bunch of Yankee road agents is gonna stop me from doin' what ah get paid tuh do.' Waco gimlet-eyed the rest of the crew. 'And ah'll ride point all the way there if these milksops who are drawin' trail-hands' pay don't feel like bein' stuck out there on the lone prairie all on their ownsome in case someone might ride up and scare them.' Waco gave them a final glare daring them to dispute his declaration then sat down.

Straight-faced Sam Ford said, 'I swear that's the most words you've strung together that made sense. You're as good as speechifying as old Abe Lincoln was, Waco.'

'Well,' Waco growled back, 'a fella's got tuh say his piece sometime.'

Phil grinned. 'The silver-tongued old goat speaks for us all, boss.' He shot a swift glance at Frank. 'And I reckon that includes cookie.'

Frank saw the relieved smile that crossed Mrs Farrow's face and thought that whatever good things he may be destined to do in his future life coming here to the Double Star to help Mrs Farrow would never be bettered. It definitely hadn't been the beer that was making him think the way he was about her. Cold sober he had the same romantic notions. And that's all they could be. Captain Farrow dead was still a hard man to replace in a woman's affections. A Yankee ploughboy hadn't a snowball's chance in hell of doing so.

'I'm glad you are willing to stay, Mr Eberhart,' Mrs Farrow said. 'But you're only new to the ranch, hired for feeding the crew not to take part in any fighting that might take place on the trail. And ...' Mrs Farrow's voice tailed away.

Frank smiled. 'And the men that I may have to fight are Yankees, like me.' His face took on a serious look. 'But that don't matter none. Killers are killers whether they be Yankees, rebs or Chinnee men, Mrs Farrow. Like Waco I'd like to say my piece, Sam.'

'You say it, boy,' Sam replied. 'You're part of the crew.'

'The way I see it,' Frank began, 'is that you'll be short-handed on the drive; the boys will have their work cut out herding the beef, making them I reckon, too tired to stand full night watches once you hit Indian territory. You can't take the risk of not being prepared for the worst, Sam.'

'You're right,' admitted Sam. 'The boys will be too played out to mount all-night guards. And the sonsuvbitches, beggin' your pardon boss, will see that and pick the time and place to jump us. They'll not take on the bigger outfits. Just what do you have in mind, Frank?'

'I'll go to Abilene,' said Frank. 'I reckon that it's

the likeliest place they'll sell the stolen cattle and the fellas that are stealing them probably spend some time in the town drinking and generally loosening up. M'be I could smell them out. I'll wear my old army tunic and put on a show as a hard-nosed Yankee loud-mouthing the day that old General Grant didn't hang Lee and Jefferson Davis for breaking up the Union.' Seeing Sam's doubtful look he added, 'I know it's a wild card I'll be playing but it's a chance, a slim one, I'll agree, and better than no chance at all. A darn sight better than sitting half-asleep in the saddle wating for a bunch of cattle-lifters to show up, Sam.'

Sam gave Frank a long thoughtful look then he said, 'I ain't a *hombre* to throw a chance away, long odds or short. You take Phil with you though Frank. If you do strike lucky and drop onto the raiders you'll need help to round them up. Texas boys. Phil can help there. I can't see a trail-boss giving a Yankee blue-belly a plate of beans let alone some of his men.'

Frank smiled across at Phil. 'That's OK by me, Sam, if Phil's willing.'

'I'm willing, Yankee,' Phil said. He grinned back at Frank. 'Some guy has to see that you don't ride straight past Kansas.'

'That will leave us two men short,' said Sam, reflectively. 'But we'll get over that somehow. And I reckon that the raiders won't be put off by having you ride with us. They'll be big enough in their own numbers to kill off eleven men as easy as nine. We'll have the pleasure of Waco doing our cooking but what the hell. If it gets us the herd safely to Abilene it will be worth it.' He grinned at the mournful-faced crew. 'I know you boys won't think so but Waco's poison ain't so permanent to a fella's well being as a dose of lead poisoning is.'

'There's no need for Waco to do the cooking, Sam,' said Mrs Farrow. 'We need him to ride point. I'll go with the herd and do the cooking.'

Sam Ford looked aghast at his boss. 'Why you can't go, boss,' he protested. 'It's nigh on five hundred miles to Abilene. There's Injuns, bad water, bad country and bad whites. Not counting them Kansas raiders. Ain't no journey for a woman at all.'

'Don't fuss so, Sam,' said Mrs Farrow, good-naturedly. 'I came to Texas from Iowa in the back of a plains wagon when I was only six years old. The wagon train had to fight off Pawnees, Kiowas and Comanche.' She smiled at her foreman. 'I know that you mean well, Sam, but don't worry on my account, you've done more than your fair share of that for me over the years. It's time I took on the full responsibility of the Double Star. Lee's future depends on it.' Mock stone-faced she added, 'And I'll be damned if I'd wish Waco's cooking on any man for more than one day. I don't want the boys to mutiny.'

'Hallelujah and amen to that, boss,' said Phil, fervently. Mrs Farrow laughed.

'Thanks for standing alongside us, Mr Eberhart,' she continued. 'Take care, and you too, Phil, there's not many of us old-hands left. I trust that I'll see you both at Abilene.' Then she left the cookhouse and the crew drifted over to the bunkhouse. Sam didn't leave with them; instead he walked across to Frank and subjected him to a keen-eyed, weighing-up look.

'Phil told me about the ruckus in Sweet Springs.

Frank. Mrs Farrow's a good woman and don't deserve being run-down by drunken assholes. Her and the captain were hardly more than kids when they first came here. Both of them worked like hell to get the place goin'. He would have been proud of her. I kinda watched out for her and the boy. Glad to know that there's someone else, outside the regular crew, feels the same way as I do about the boss.'

'Sit down, Sam,' said Frank, and poured out a cup of coffee for the foreman. 'I think that you oughta know why I came to the Double Star. I've been waiting for the right moment to tell someone. I reckon that moment has come, just in case I don't make it back from Abilene. It was like this, at Chickamaugo ...'

'Well I'll be durned,' breathed Sam. 'Well, I'll be ...' So engrossed in Frank's story that his coffee lay cold and untouched.

'What's been chewing at me, Sam,' Frank added, 'is I lack the nerve to tell Mrs Farrow about it, and she's the one that should be told. Could you tell her and give her the captain's watch and the letters after I ride out?'

Sam shook his head. 'It's not that I wouldn't do it, boy but I think that it's you that has to do the telling. And you know it. Mrs Farrow deserves better treatment than hearing about the death of her husband second-hand. You go and do what you came here for; I'll give Phil a hand to saddle up your horse and fix you up with provisions.'

'Yeah, you're right, Sam,' said Frank. 'It has to be me.' He took off his cook's apron. 'And right now; I've delayed speaking out long enough. I'll go across to the bunkhouse and pick up the watch and the letter, finish up here afterwards.' Teeth gritted resolutely he left the cookhouse leaving Sam still thinking how peoples' fates get crossed. Luck? The Indians put it down as a man's destiny, all written down in a book of life just waiting to happen. Whatever it was Sam opined he was glad that Mr Eberhart had felt that it was some part of his destiny to make the trip to the Double Star. What he had to relate would give Mrs Farrow peace of mind at last.

'Is that Pa's watch, Mum?' Lee asked.

Mrs Farrow smiled gently at her son. 'Yes it is, Lee. And we thought that we would never see it again. Now it is yours.'

Frank was sitting opposite them in the parlour of the ranch-house. Haltingly at first he began telling her how her husband had met his death. Then seeing the quiet calmness of Mrs Farrow as she listened, the apprehensions he had held about having one day to face the captain's widow vanished and the words came flooding out.

'I felt beholden to you to bring back the captain's personal effects, ma'am,' he said. 'I didn't read the letters, well, only to find out who the captain was so that I could pay my respects to his kin.'

Mrs Farrow handed the watch to Lee then, sad, sweet-smiling she began reading one of the letters. Frank made to get up, to leave Mrs Farrow to share her memories and sorrow with her son as he thought was right. He had no business taking part in her private grief.

'No, don't go, Mr Eberhart,' Mrs Farrow said. 'Please stay awhile.'

Surprised Frank sank back into his chair. Mrs

Farrow smiled her thanks. She felt no bitterness towards Mr Eberhart, that he was sitting in the chair alive, instead of her husband. She felt she was more at peace with herself than at any time since she had heard of James's death. James, even at the end, had done what he knew to be right. No matter how much she missed him she couldn't find fault with James for putting what his conscience told him to do before his own safety and his return to her and Lee, and saving Mr Eberhart from a terrible death. Somehow, she couldn't rightly understand why, Mr Eberhart was filling part of the emptiness within her. Feeling just for a brief moment that it was James sitting there.

Lee opened the watch and looked at the inscription inside.

'Your pa was a real hero, Lee,' Frank told him. 'Anyone can be a bit of a hero when his dander's up and he's chargin' along with the rest of the boys. But your pa went out of his way to save an enemy solider, me, and paid for it with his own life.' He looked at Mrs Farrow. 'M'be it's foolish for me to say so, ma'am, but if a man has to die in battle the captain couldn't have picked a better way to go. Not killing but saving life and dying quickly with no pain. I hope that's of some comfort to you, ma'am.'

Mrs Farrow got up from her chair and leaning across kissed Frank on the cheek. Impulsively, yet knowing that it was what he had to do, he put his hands on her shoulders and stood up, bringing her up with him. Pulling her close he held her tight against him, feeling the wetness on her cheeks as her face brushed his. Silently he shared her sorrow and held her to him till he felt Mrs Farrow's body stop its heartrending shuddering and trembling.

Mrs Farrow slowly drew herself away and Frank let his arms drop to his sides. Smiling through her tears Mrs Farrow said, 'Thanks for telling me, Mr Eberhart.' Her gaze dropped away from his and Frank saw colour coming back into her face. 'And for holding me. I'll be all right now; with your help I've finally laid James to rest in my mind. I can look forward to building a future for Lee. You take care of yourself, Mr Eberhart, in Kansas and take care of Phil. He's been with me since James and me started to build up the ranch. And the poor boy has suffered enough.'

'I'll do that, Mrs Farrow,' replied Frank. 'And you look out for yourself; it will be no picnic on the trail for you. I'll see you in Abilene.' Providing the drive didn't hit trouble on the trail he sombrely thought.

Mrs Farrow wanted to ask him if he intended to return to the ranch once the cattle had been sold. She hoped that he would. It would be only hope for Mr Eberhart had done his duty as he saw it by leaving his family to tell her about James. She felt that she couldn't ask him for more of his life however much she desired it. He had his own family and their commitments to tend to.

Sam Ford, Mrs Farrow and Lee stood on the porch watching Frank and Phil ride off. Sam, noticing the look that Mrs Farrow gave Frank, grunted with satisfaction. He opined that she could be thinking and feeling that maybe it was time that she shared her life with another man, not only for Lee's sake. Frank's expression was that he would be in favour of a closer relationship with the boss if she got round to hinting at it. One thing was for sure, the captain wouldn't want either of them

denied their happiness together just for the sake of
his memory. He hoped that the big Yankee would
still be around when they reached Abilene. Having
another man she cared for going to an early grave
would be too much for the boss to handle. And he
couldn't be father and uncle to her and Lee
forever.

SIX

Mort Dunstan, a short round-faced individual, gazed benignly from behind the crowded long bar of the Texas Drover Saloon; A genuine picture of a saloon owner smirking with pleasure at the sight of his bar bursting at the seams with hard-drinking customers. The inner truth was much different. Mort hated the guts of every one of the Texans drinking in his saloon. Like Captain Hardin he didn't accept that the war was over. By his reckoning he still had a long way to go before he evened up his personal score against the former Confederates.

Unlike Captain Hardin he didn't want their blood as well as their cattle. He was quite content taking their hard-earned pay from them for the snake juice he palmed off as real drinking man's whiskey, the fixed gambling tables, plus the cut he received from the captain when the stolen cattle were sold. Mort's pasted-on smile slipped slightly. The sons-of-bitches hadn't paid in full yet, not by a long streak. When he thought about it it seemed that it all happened yesterday, but eleven years and a big war had gone by since the Border Ruffians crossed over from Missouri and put the free-soil township of Lawrence to the torch.

The Dunstan family had title to property and land, good bottom land dirt, near Lawrence. Pa, his brother, Luther, and him had worked their balls off clearing and ploughing the land till the farm brought enough in to see to their needs and a piece left over for when he and Luther felt it was time to take it easy and retire to the rocking chairs on the front porch and pay hired hands to do the hard chores, Pa and Ma lying peaceful in their graves by then.

Kansas in '55 was a free-soil, anti-slave state but Mort blew neither way on the issue that would split the Union apart. If a man felt he had the right to own slaves so be it. If another man reckoned that it was his divine duty to free those slaves, shed his own blood, and others' doing so, well good luck to him Mort thought, as long as the blood shed was long ways from the Dunstan farm. The Missouri guerillas brought the blood spilling right to his front porch. After raiding Lawrence they burnt down every homestead they passed on the way back to Missouri.

Mort had been away from the farm all day and on the ride back he smelt smoke. That gave him foreboding of what he would see when he dropped down into the valley. But only a taste. His cup of bitterness came brimming full when he saw the bodies of his pa and Luther swinging from a branch of the oak tree and found his mother lying dead from what he opined was a heart attack at the terrible sight she had witnessed. The house was too engulfed in flames for him to do anything but let it burn.

Mort, after decently burying his family, sat down and cried long and bitterly. Some of the tears were shed for the loss of his close kin and the love he naturally felt for them. The big tears were for himself. Without his pa and Luther he would never be able to build up the farm to the richness it had been. Gone was his comfortable old age with the whiskey jug and his pipe. The tears were of anger at the thought that the pro-slaver sons-of-bitches had ruined him. From that day on Mort came off the fence and declared his undying support for the abolitionist cause, joining the scourge of the Missourian border homesteads, Colonel Lane's "Red Leg" guerillas.

After the big war Mort stayed on with Captain Hardin and the rest of the men who wanted to continue with their wartime raiding and stealing. There wasn't much else ex-guerillas with prices on their heads could turn their hands to to feed and clothe themselves. Mort, a lot richer than he was when he went to war, no longer rode out on raiding trips. He owned a ranch near the town as well as the Texas Drover; well placed to ship the stolen cattle through the pens with his own stock.

The ranch was also used as a hole-up for the gang in between raids. If they felt the pressing urge for female companionship or a few glasses of beer they would drift into Abilene and the Texas Drover in their twos and threes so as not to attract the attention of any army patrol that might be snooping around. Many of the citizens of Abilene presented no threat to the marauders. The Texans still being no-good rebs to their way of thinking, they wished the "brush boys" good luck in their owlhooting enterprises.

Extra loud shouts and the sounds of breaking glass cut into Mort's chain of thoughts. He picked up the double-barrelled shotgun from a shelf beneath the bar. Still showing his fixed grin he pointed the gun at the four Texans exchanging blows and oaths. 'Now, boys, whatever it is that's got you all het up just go and sort it out in the street or this gun is liable to go off. And just think of the mess your blood will make on my floor.' Mort raised his voice into a bull-like roar. 'Drinks on the house, gents!' he called.

The struggling trail-hands were pushed aside by the mass rush to the bar to take up the offer. Mort cursed under his breath all the while he was smiling as he watched his sweating barkeeps pouring out the free drinks. Yet he had to admit that a dozen or so bottles of cheap redeye was a small price to pay for not getting his place wrecked. If he had used the shotgun the Texans would have drawn their big Colts and the war would have started all over again.

He would have to bend the mayor's ear about appointing a town sheriff to curb the wilder spirits among the trail-hands. The man would have to be a real fearless, hard-nosed son-of-a-bitch to uphold the law in Abilene during the trailing season; one with a real gut-hatred for Texans, like him and Captain Hardin, for the pay he would get for wearing a tin star wasn't a lot for a man to lay his life on the line facing up to the wild-assed bastards when they were baying at the moon.

SEVEN

Frank and Phil were real *compadres* when they made camp just short of the Red River. Another day's riding would see them in the badlands of the Nations, marauder and hostile Indian territory. On the ride up from the Brazos Phil became more sociable, telling Frank of the early days on the ranch. How he and Chris went off to the war with Captain Farrow leaving old man Ford and Mrs Farrow and a few Mexican *vaqueros* to run the ranch. Chris had been the lucky one. He had returned to the ranch with no bits missing. He'd left an eye and the best part of an arm at the fighting at Yellow Tavern trying to stop Sherman's boys fireballing it down the Shenandoah Valley, the very day General Jeb Stuart got himself killed.

Frank related how Captain Farrow had saved his life at Chickamaugo and its honour-bound outcome. At the news Phil, though he had taken a liking to Frank since the fight with the drunks at Sweet Springs, took to Frank as he would to a brother. He knew that not many men had it in them to come this far to fulfil a promise made in the heat of battle to a dead enemy two years back. He hoped to hell that he would not let Frank down when the shit began to fly. He had to forget that he was only a one-eyed, one-armed kid. But the last time trouble hit him he had a whole regiment alongside him and could handle a rifle and still lost out.

To meet any tight situation he and Frank found themselves in, he had only a six-load pistol to help them out, and another eye and a arm to give if needs be. Without being too pessimistic Phil reckoned that if they did cross trails with the cattle lifters the pair of them would need all the luck that was going to come out alive.

'When we cross the Red,' Frank said, 'we'll start out as what we're supposed to be. I'll wear my blue-belly tunic; you'll be a Texan that fought for the Union returning from a visit to your folks that nearly ended up, if I hadn't been around, in you getting run out of town on a pole all nicely tarred and feathered for being a sonuvabitch turncoat. It won't do to take any chances, Phil, the gang's bound to have men out keeping a watch on the trail, picking out likely herds to raid.'

'Yeah,' Phil said. 'We're just a coupla war buddies that fought at Chickamaugo Creek together. Me being an all-shot-up cripple you're kinda lookin' out for me. Help me to get on to my horse, see to my pants when I come off the crapper.'

Frank grinned. 'If that heart-rending tale don't swing things our way then we'll just have to get the drop on the nosy bastards.'

They had passed two herds on the way to the Red and came across another fording the river. Frank pulled his horse to a halt and took in the scene of several hundred bawling longhorns splashing belly-deep through the shallows, chivvied along by the whoops and yells of the trail-hands and their high-stepping spray-raising ponies.

'When the Double Star starts out, Phil,' Frank said as the young Texan drew up alongside him, 'every longhorn in the state of Texas must be heading for Kansas.'

Phil grinned. 'What do you expect, Yankee, when a steer worth five dollars in Texas is worth fifty in Abilene? A rancher will be prepared to face the devil himself for that sort of return on his stock. Why if it wasn't for those critters down there in the water the state of Texas would be plumb broke, and that's a fact.'

'It's no wonder the herds get raided,' said Frank. 'It's a darn sight quicker way of raisin' cash than digging for gold.'

They crossed the river well clear of the organized chaos at the ford and rode till they reached the herd's cook's wagon, drawn up behind a fold in the ground a mile or so ahead of the main herd. Several trail-hands were standing round the wagon drinking coffee and drawing on their makings. The pair of them were given the fish-eyed treatment as they rode up. The hard suspicious looks faded somewhat and hands lifted off gun butts as the tension eased when they saw that one of the strangers was missing an arm and an eye.

The cold reception disappeared altogether when Phil, still mounted, told them that they worked for Mrs Farrow of the Double Star ranch back in Brazo County. He spun the trail-hands a yarn about how they were on their way to Abilene to buy some horses for Mrs Farrow as half of their remuda had picked up some sort of sickness and wouldn't last out the long haul to Abilene. The trail-boss, a tall, gangling-limbed man, invited them to step down and share in what vittles there were on offer. Phil grinned at Frank as he slipped off his horse. Low-voiced he said, 'I hope the cook ain't kin to Waco.'

'Bad country up ahead,' the trail-boss told them as they were drinking their coffee. 'For two men, one not whole – no offence, kid – to be riding across. There's Injuns out there, one of my point riders cut sign of a bunch of them headin' eastwards just before we began sending the beef across the Red. Now I hear that there're some former Kansas brush boys that don't think the war is over raidin' Texas herds.' The tall man gave them a mirthless undertaker's smile. 'If those sonsuvbitches try and lift the Bar X cattle they'll find out for sure that the war ain't ended. It's safer for you boys to tag along with the outfit, but do what you think's best, Mrs Farrow pays your wages and you're doin' her business.'

It was good common, self-preservation sense Frank opined for the Texans to be prepared for trouble and reckoned that being only two of them was the reason for him and Phil being allowed to approach the camp. A bunch of riders would have been denied that invitation in no uncertain terms, from the ready-to-use gun muzzles. He soberly thought that if he'd been wearing his army tunic his and Phil's ride to Abilene would have ended a rifle shot's distance from where he was standing.

Frank thanked the trail-boss but told him that they would have to take a chance on running into trouble along the trail. Their orders had been to get to Abilene fast and return just as fast with the horses to the herd, four herds back down the trail, before the crew had to tend to longhorns on foot, he lyingly told him. It certainly wouldn't be wise for a man that was passing himself off as a hard-nosed reb hater to even be seen passing the time of day with Texans. Riding alongside them, sharing their rations would destroy that image altogether if word got round in Abilene that the big blue-belly had been herding Texas beef. It would prevent him him from getting any closer to the Hardin gang than he was right now. It also could get him dead.

They said their farewells then mounted their horses. Phil with a quick cat-like spring as though he was getting astride a bare-backed Indian pony. He gave the trail-hands a wide-open, cocky grin. 'If any of you *hombres* make it to Abilene I'll stand you a drink.' He looked across to the trail-boss. 'That's if only half a man can get himself there, no offence, boss.'

The trail-boss grinned back. 'Why you young sonuvabitch,' he said, his smile in his voice. 'I'll hold you to it.' He glanced at Frank wondering why a man that spoke like a Yankee pardnered a half-pint crippled Texan kid but he kept his curiosity to himself. All he said was, 'I don't know who's looking out for who but both of you take care and if you're lucky enough to make it back to the Widow Farrow give her my regards.'

They pulled in beneath a rocky overhang that sheltered them from the cool wind that began to blow across the flats as the red ball of fire that was the sun dipped below the far rim of the plains. Phil suggested that they make a cold camp. Lighting fires could attract the unwelcome attention of the band of hostiles that the trail-boss had mentioned were roaming somewhere about the territory.

'We don't want bare-assed hostiles to come sneaking up on us, Frank,' he said. 'Hostiles with pants on, like Capt'n Hardin and his bully boys are more than enough for a Yankee ploughboy and a crippled kid to take on. Did you have Injun trouble in Minnesota, Frank?' Phil asked.

'Trouble?' replied Frank. 'No, no trouble, Phil. But we did have a real big war with the Sioux back in '62.' He grinned. 'It wasn't all sodbusting back home. The Sioux don't ride out to do their killing and burning in dozens. When they break out they raise a whole damn light cavalry brigade. And it nigh took an army to herd them back to the agency. I would reckon that counts for little more than just Indian trouble, wouldn't you, Phil?'

Phil, as he turned over to go to sleep, thought that Frank, a man who had fought the bloodthirsty Sioux and Texans and could still smile when he spoke of it, was a man who had true grit. Good enough to be a Texan. 'Good night, Frank,' he said. But Frank was already asleep.

Frank felt himself being shaken by the shoulders. Instantly he came awake and made a grab for his pistol lying at his side. His dreams of the sweet-smiling Isobel Farrow and the part he would like her to play in his future gone like the phantasies they were. Phil put a warning finger to his mouth. 'Listen,' he said.

The moon hadn't risen yet and only the stars lit up the blue-black arc of the sky. The wind had dropped and Frank could clearly hear the noise that had alerted Phil, the creaking of saddle leather and the sharp striking sound of a horse's foot stumbling on a rock on the trail they'd pulled off to make camp.

'Indians?' asked Frank.

Phil shook his head. 'Not unless bucks are takin' to ride ponies that have saddles and iron-shod hooves. Ain't trail-hands either. If they were they'd be talking their heads off. Besides there ain't no herd within' thirty miles of here.'

'That only leaves Captain Hardin and his crew,' said Frank.

'Looks like it,' Phil answered. 'And I reckon that the no-good trash are sneakin' down the trail to raid the Bar X.'

'I wouldn't disagree with that reckoning,' said Frank as he got to his feet and began buckling on his pistol belt. 'We sure can't surround them and call on the sonsuvbitches to throw down their guns but we can give the Bar X a hand in spoiling the captain's thieving intentions. And if we get lucky, m'be kill a few of the bastards.'

Captain Hardin lifted a white gloved hand and the double file of riders broke column and fanned out in a line either side of him. Riders ass-shuffled in nervous anticipation, waiting for the captain's word that would send them riding into the trail-hands' camp, quiet and peaceful as a graveyard, slowly at first then clearing the last hundred yards in a wild ass-kicking yelling and shooting gallop.

Captain Hardin gave the silent camp a long calculating look. Earlier one of his scouts had reported back that the herd that was crossing the Red was manned by a big crew and would have in his opinion a double shift of night riders out. Too many for Tod to creep round on his belly slitting their throats. It was to be expected the captain thought that after the first few raids the Texans would naturally strengthen their crews but he also reckoned that he still had a slight edge, a swift and all out attack.

Men can't be on their mettle twenty-four hours a day, not after at least two-thirds of those hours were spent hard-assing it in the saddle herding the longhorns. It would be like it was in the old days: ride in fast, kill fast.

Once they hit the camp Sergeant Kegg and his men would peel off and go for the cattle. He would see to it that the men not shot down in their first sweep of the camp were too busy fighting to stay alive to be concerned about some stinking longhorns being lifted. The captain smiled his steel-cold grin of satisfaction. He could see no hitch to his plan. It wasn't like they were riding in against well-dug entrenchments or strongly-fortified redoubts. Half asleep dollar-a-day saddlebums, rolling out of blankets, boots off, suspender entangled legs, weren't as steady under fire in a surprise night attack as regular soldier boys.

Frank and Phil, dismounted and crouched low down, picked out the line of horsemen against the star-filled sky. Frank halted and putting a hand on Phil's shoulder whispered, 'Move out to your left and when I start to fire come in slow towards me, OK? I'll move to my right. I want them to think there's a lot of us. But keep your head down because when the Bar X boys cut loose with their guns there's going to be a real storm of lead coming in this direction.'

'If you're reckonin' to start a small battle, Frank,' Phil said.'Remember I've only got six loads. And I can't see me kneeling down gripping my Colt with my kneecaps trying to thumb in fresh loads in the dark and getting shot at I ain't that steady nerved.'

'Sorry,' said Frank and he handed Phil his own pistol. 'Stick that down your pants top, I'll use my rifle. One thing more, if those raiders scatter this way get down low, understand? We're only here to cause a little confusion, and drop one or two of them, not to take on the whole bunch.' He added to himself that he very much wanted to stay alive to see Mrs Farrow again.

Frank waited, wound up tight, till Phil had slithered crabwise out of his sight. It might be only a small shoot-out but he was feeling that he was back in the railroad cutting at Chickamaugo waiting for the whole reb army to attack. He waited a few seconds more for Phil to get into position before bringing up his rifle, aiming, and pulling off a load. He saw one of the shadowy figures drop from his horse then swung his rifle on to another target. He heard Phil's bubbling, blood-curdling rebel yell, a sound that still raised the hairs at the back of his neck, then the single spaced cracks of his Colt. Frank stepped a few paces to his right, took aim again, fired. Then all hell broke loose.

Gun flashes broke the darkness at the trail-herders' camp and the raiders suffered more casualties. They began to return the fire, wildly aimed, shooting at the camp and at the unexpected threat from their rear. The surprisers had become the surprised. The captain subscribed to the military maxim that when you're in a tight spot it's wiser to cut your losses and get to hell out of it but fast. You can always try and grab the other fella's balls another day.

'Pull out men!' he yelled above the roar of the guns.

Frank saw the dark wall of horsemen pounding towards him and he flung himself to the ground. One horse thundered past him so close that he was showered with stones and dirt kicked up by its speeding hooves. Frank raised himself up a little and snapped off a shot at its rider. He saw the man sway in his saddle before vanishing in the darkness. Frank reckoned with some satisfaction that he had hit the man high, in the right shoulder he calculated.

Phil joined him, grinning joyfully like a man that's laid his first woman. 'We sure scared the hell outa those Kansas boys, Frank,' he said. Then frantically splayed himself on the ground alongside Frank as a burst of rifle fire from the camp sent a hail of lead whizzing over their heads. Phil cursed. Losing his grin he yelled, 'You dimwitted assholes, hold your fire! It's me! the one-armed kid! The raiders have gone!' He got to his feet. 'There's two of us comin' in so take the pressure off your trigger fingers. The Yankees tried hard to kill me during the war, I don't take kindly to Texans figurin' to do likewise.'

'This is the second time I'm gonna have to bid you two pilgrims farewell,' the trail-boss said, eyeing Frank and Phil speculatively. 'I ain't that nosy as to ask you why you should have been where you were instead of being well along the trail to Abilene to buy those horses your boss lady so urgently needs. Not that I ain't right glad that you showed up when you did. We were ready for those bastards but it would have been a damned hard fight to have held them off without some of my boys getting hurt real bad.' The trail-boss reached out and shook Frank and Phil's hands. 'My handle is Luke Dolan, straw boss of this outfit in case you ain't guessed. M'be some day I can do you boys a favour, I'm owin' to you.'

Frank looked at Phil before speaking. Phil deciphering Frank's silent thoughts nodded his head in agreement. 'You go and tell him, Frank. We ain't a coupla town-tamers, we m'be could use all the help we can get.'

'It's like this, Mr Dolan,' Frank began. 'I'm the cook of the Double Star, Frank Eberhart, and when we heard about the cattle raids me and Phil here got this crazy notion ...'

Luke Dolan listened with open-mouthed intensity as Frank told him of his plan of action on reaching Abilene. When he finished he said, 'Your idea wasn't as way out as you thought, Mr Eberhart. How, I don't rightly know, but you did meet up with the cattle lifters a lot faster I reckon than you expected to. And helped us to beat the sonsuvbitches off.' He grinned at Frank. 'My cook don't get any ideas at all, crazy or otherwise. You should get an easy ride to Abilene now as I think that the captain will take a little time off his raidin' schedule and hole-up somewhere so he can lick his wounds. The boys have just brung in four dead and one half dead.' Luke Dolan's grin lacked warmth this time round. 'The thieving asshole will be real dead the first stout tree we come to. Don't forget, Mr Eberhart, if you want help when we reach town just keep lookin' in the bars or the whorehouses till you find us. We may look a little different when we're washed and dressed up for the occasion but you'll recognize our homely mugs and we'll come a-runnin'.'

Frank, after they had put some ground between

them and the trail-herders' camp, did what he had
told Phil he intended doing before they crossed the
Red, he put on his army jacket.

'Mr Dolan m'be right about Captain Hardin
holing-up, Phil,' he said. 'but as I said it don't do to
take chances. The sonsuvbitches could be still
roaming about over the next ridge, wild and
mean-tempered at losing out. Liable to come down
on anyone they see just to get rid of all that
ill-feeling they must be carrying around. The
captain reckons that he's still fighting for the
Union. That loyalty might prevent him from
plugging a man that's wearing a blue-belly coat.'

Frank finished buttoning up his jacket then said,
'OK, Phil, let's get us to Abilene and see if we can
meet up with the captain and his boys again, at our
doing, with plenty of backup.'

Sam Ford stood up in his stirrups and gave one
quick but expert glance at the postion of the flank
riders ringing the herd. Satisfied, he sat back in the
saddle and rode to where Waco, ready to move out
as point rider, was waiting. He drew up alongside
him and pointed with his chin to the cook's wagon
rumbling along the trail several hundred yards
ahead.

'Keep an eye on the boss, Waco,' he said. 'I know
Blue's with her but the kid's never been more than
a gunshot away from Sweet Springs before. He's
liable to turn the wagon round and finish up on the
Rio Grande.'

'Sure thing,' replied Waco.

'OK then, let's get this circus on the road,' Sam
said.

Waco dug his heels into his horse's flanks and

followed in the dust wake of the cook's wagon. Sam twisted round in his saddle and took a final look at the herd. He tried to think no further ahead than the first night camp, reflecting that taking the Double Star cattle to Kansas was not one of the sanest things he had taken on in his life. He knew that he hadn't the most experienced crew in Texas, a lot was riding on a big Yankee ploughboy and a crippled kid. What the hell, he thought. If the captain was still in the cattle-raiding business it didn't mean that he was going to pick on the Double Star beef. There were plenty other herds on the trail for the marauders to raid. Sam tried to convince himself that he was worrying and fretting over nothing like some old woman. It could be, but a gut feeling was telling him that long odds have a habit of coming up when least expected. Passing another what-to-hell thought Sam cupped his hands to his mouth and bellowed, 'OK, amigos! Let's move 'em out!' High pitched rebel yells echoed his shout then came the bellowing and snorting as the longhorns, hooves kicking up the dust, took their first steps on the long trail to the railhead.

Isobel Farrow heard the noise and smiled at Blue. 'At last we are on our way,' she said. Yet her mind wasn't entirely full of the excitement and feeling of accomplishment of a rancher, a woman, leading her first herd to Kansas. Part of her was thinking about Mr Eberhart and what danger he and Phil could be putting themselves in on her behalf. She was afraid that those disturbing thoughts were going to give her some long, worrying days and nights on the journey ahead. All she could do was to pray for their safety.

EIGHT

Mayor Bailey gave Deputy State Marshal Calder a cold-eyed look from across his desk. 'But you've got to do something about it, Marshal. You're supposed to represent the law,' he angrily insisted. 'All the saloon owners are at me, the trail-hands are smashing their places up in drunken orgies.'

'You should tell the saloon owners to sell a better class of liquor,' the marshal replied. 'The poison that they sell would turn a sky pilot into a blood-thirty bronco. I can't trail all the way down here from the State capital every time there's a disturbance in some bar or other. I've got more than my hands full trying to track down Captain Hardin and his gang and several other owlhoot bands that operate in the territory. You just elect a good man as town sheriff and you'll soon find that the little upsets the saloon owners are beefing about will end.' The marshal favoured the mayor with a fatherly, I-know-best look, though thinking that the mealy-mouthed asshole was all for the railroad running a line here to Abilene; welcomed the trail-hands with open arms so that they could spend their hard-earned dollars in the town. The saloon owners and the cathouse madams couldn't separate the Texans from their cash fast enough.

Now that the boys were acting up a mite boisterous, a few glasses broken, tables and chairs bust up they come crying to the law for help. Marshal Calder, if he hadn't reckoned himself to be a gentleman, would have spat on the highly-polished floor-boards of the mayor's office in disgust.

Mayor Bailey's face got a deeper red. 'We had a sheriff but as soon as he saw the dust of the first trailherd nearing the town he handed in his badge. Said he had a belly full of fighting Texans during the war without starting it all over again.'

'Sorry I can't find the time to help you out, Mayor,' said the marshal, pulling himself up off his chair. 'But it's a local lawman you want, a town-tamer. Or tell those saloon owners to sell soda pop instead of that moonshine they dish out.' Marshal Calder grinned lewdly. 'Or tell those cathouse madams to import some fresh hot-assed talent in so that the boys get real tuckered out, too dead beat to do anything but sit and down their liquor and have an early night in bed.' The marshal glanced idly out of the mayor's office window. 'Now that big guy pulling up outside the livery bar has the makin's of a town-tamer to ride into a burg that's bustin' at the seams with the late Stonewall Jackson's veterans wearing a blue-belly's jacket all proud like.'

The mayor eased his portly bulk from behind his desk and hurried across the room to take a look at a possible straw he could grab hold of to get the saloon owners off his back. Liking what he saw he made to go to the door but the marshal laid a restraining hand on his shoulder.

'Take it easy, Mayor,' he said. 'You don't know who the big fella is. It ain't a candy bar you're tryin' to get him to take. Could be flyers posted out for his arrest. Kansas is full of bad-asses, former blue-bellies and rebs, unable to settle down again at the back of the plough after all the killin' they've seen and done. Keep an eye on him for a day or two; see if he intends staying in town. Meanwhile I'll check out the wanted flyers in my office to see if I've got anything on someone that fits his description. I'll let you know as soon as I can if he's clean enough to wear a tin star.'

Frank tied up his horse outside the stables and walked inside to see to it that his horse got attended to. He had split up with Phil, at his insistence, on the edge of town, telling him how he saw things and the way he was going to play them out. He had told Phil to drop his role as a pro-Union Texan.

'I don't want you getting into trouble with your fellow Texans,' he said. 'We were only after foolin' Captain Hardin; there's no need for that trick now.'

'What the hell am I supposed to do?' protested Phil. 'I ain't hard-assed it all this way just to stand drinking in some bar or whorehouse. You can get yourself in real trouble as well, Frank. The Texans won't take kindly to you hassling them; and being on your own they'll stomp you in the ground.'

'I was thinking about that, Phil,' replied Frank. 'It don't seem all that good of an idea as it did back at the Double Star. M'be I should stick to sounding off how I suppose to feel about you Johnny Rebs in front of the locals. Could be that one of them might relate that he knows where a bunch of similar thinking men hang out.' Frank gave a wry grin and shrugged his shoulders. 'It sure isn't much of a plan but it's all I can come up with and we've got to try it, Phil. It don't bear thinking about what would happen to Mrs Furrow and the boys if those bastards take it in their minds to raid the Double Star herd.'

'Yeah, I suppose that's the way you've got to play it,' a still nettled Phil grudgingly admitted. 'but you ain't told me what I'm expected to do.'

Frank smiled at him. 'Calm down, kid. If I meet up with Captain Hardin I'll need help, lots of it. I'll contact you, then you can round up Luke Dolan and his crew, if they're in Abilene, or any other crew that fancies settling up with the gang that's raiding their herds for good. From now on in we can't be seen together, but keep a close eye on me. We're trying to fool men that are not easily conned and don't lose any sleep over killing men that get in their way.'

'Well,' said Phil, seeing the logic of Frank's reasoning at last. 'I guess that's the only choice we've got. I'll stick to you as close as I can without giving any nosy sonuvabitch an inkling that we're in cahoots. But go easy on riling the trail-hands, they're a wild, untamed bunch of *hombres*. They're m'be rough but they've still got their pride. And that, Mr Eberhart,' Phil added seriously, 'is a fact, for I'm one of them.'

Two hours later, after booking himself a room in one of the town's many boarding-houses, Phil picking a different one, Frank walked along Main Street towards the south of tracks, saloon and bawdy house section of Abilene. He had to try out his so-called plan, as he reckoned by now the Double Star herd would be on the trail. Frank's face steeled over; easy prey for Captain Hardin and his gang. Where they were was something he had to find out fast for time wasn't on his side. And he hadn't come all the way south just to fail Mrs Farrow on the first real chance he had of helping her. There was also his pride to think about. He'd be damned before he'd head back to Minnesota with his tail between his legs like a whipped cur dog, that or dead. He noticed Phil strolling along on the opposite boardwalk. He smiled slightly. the kid was taking his part of the plan seriously. A sallow-faced, pot-bellied man in a dark suit standing outside a store that bore the legend, *The Trail-End Dry Goods Store,* painted on a board that hung on chains above the window, greeted Frank with a cheerful. 'Good afternoon, sir.' Mayor Bailey was after having a closer look at the possible next sheriff of Abilene.

Frank paused in his stride and touched his hat in reply to the mayor's greeting. 'And to you, sir,' he added.

Mayor Bailey smiled. 'It's good to see the old uniform again, sir.' His smile clouded over. 'Unfortunately I was too old to do any actual fighting but like the rest of the citizens of Abilene I fully supported the Union cause. Helped to raise a lot of cash to buy comforts for the brave sons of the town that bore arms against the rebs.'

Frank opined that the garrulous old goat's professed sadness and disappointment at not being able to risk life and limb, shed his rich red blood in the defence of the Union was as sincere as his oily smile of welcome. Why the storekeeper had picked him to hold a conversation with he didn't know. At least it had broken the ice for him in Abilene and it would be the gabby ones who would be the more likely to let slip any information about the whereabouts of Captain Hardin.

Before Frank could carry on with the conversation Phil brushed past him, deliberately nudging him sharply in the ribs and snarling, 'Do you blasted nigra-lovin' blue-bellies think you own the boardwalk?'

Frank, holding back his smile, twisted his face in supposed anger. Addressing the mayor he said caustically, 'I didn't think that the Union-backing citizens of Abilene would allow secessionists to walk the streets as though they'd won the war. Why if that traitor hadn't been a crippled kid I would have called him out and shot him down like the way we did to his slave owning brethren at Chickamauga.'

Mayor Bailey gave Frank a weak apologetic grin. 'One of the crosses we have to bear for Abilene being a trail-end town.' He was thinking that by what he had just heard the big Yankee held no fear of the Texans and their wild ways one little bit. He was, he reckoned, gazing at a tailor-made lawman for Abilene. Of course the boy would have to be calmed down somewhat. He couldn't go shooting the ears off every Texan that rubbed him up the wrong way; the town's citizens wouldn't stand for Abilene turned into another Gettysburg, but he could have a free hand in dealing with the assholes that started any fights in the saloons. And he would have to stop wearing that jacket. His blue-belly coat with a tin star pinned on it would bring the trail-hands' blood to the boil faster than Mort Dunstan's rotgut whiskey did.

'Yeah, m'be so,' Frank replied. 'But it sure riles a man to see them parading about like fighting cocks.'

'A good peace officer would keep them in line,' the mayor said, trailing his first tentative line. 'I'm

Mayor Bailey and you intend staying in town, mister, …?

'Frank Eberhart,' Frank said. 'All the way from Minnesota.'

'Well, as I was saying, Mr Eberhart,' the mayor continued, 'if you are staying any length of time in Abilene there's more than a fair chance that I could fix you up with a job.' The mayor's skin-deep smile blossomed again. 'It's the least I can do for one of General Grant's veterans.' The mayor was all set to put the sheriff's badge in Frank's hand there and then and to hell with waiting for Marshal Calder's sayso. He held back from doing so realizing that he couldn't just spring the news on a complete stranger that he'd been elected sheriff of Abilene without his by your leave. There was no sense in frightening him away. Let him get the feel of the town first, have a few beers, a woman, to soften him a little. Mort Dunstan could wait another day or so for his sheriff.

'Why thank you, Mayor,' replied Frank. 'I reckoned on staying in town a while but most of the work I can see being done around the place is to do with cattle, and I'm not a cattleman. So any other job of work will be much appreciated.' Frank thought that it was time he made his prejudices known to the mayor if he hadn't already got the message. 'I suppose I'll just have to get used to having rebs around me but by thunder if any of them that has all his limbs gives me any sass so help me I'll …'

Mayor Bailey couldn't stop himself from shuddering as he saw the scowling, hard-faced Indian-like expression that came over Mr Eberhart's face. Without doubt he was facing a real mean son-of-a-bitch town-tamer.

'Where are you staying, Mr Eberhart?' he asked.

'I've a room in a boarding-house a couple blocks back along the street,' Frank told him.

'Ah, Mrs Leigh's place,' the mayor said. 'You'll be comfortable there, good food and clean beds. I'll leave a message for you there when I've got your job fixed up. Now I won't detain you any longer, Mr Eberhart, it's been a pleasure to make your acquaintance.' The mayor switched on his false smile once more. 'If you are wishing to partake of a beer or something stronger then you need not venture any further than the Texas Drover saloon across the street there. Knowing your firmly stated views, Mr Eberhart I reckon tht the name won't please you any but Mr Mort Dunstan will see you right. Tell him I sent you.'

'I'll do just that,' said Frank. 'And thanks for putting a job my way.' He saluted the mayor as a farewell gesture, thinking as he strode across the street to the saloon at least he wouldn't starve while he was doing his snooping around. He would have to see to it that Phil had enough money to get by.

There were only seven customers in the Texas Drover when Frank pushed through the swing doors. Two elderly trail-hands, seemingly by their pale washed-out visages, partaking of the hair of the dog, and Phil were at the bar. At a table near the door sat three men who Frank thought were local boys discussing some deal or other. The seventh customer, a snappily dressed, smooth-faced man with a drummer's carpet bag resting on the floor by his feet was exchanging pleasantries with a red-haired girl. Behind the bar a shirt-sleeved man, wearing a fancy vest, stood with his elbows resting on the bar top chewing at the end of a cigar. Frank took him to be Mort Dunstan, the owner of the saloon.

At his entrance all the customers, excepting the two trail-hands with the hangovers, glanced in his direction. Mort and Julie, the redhead, giving the new customer more than a cursory empty-eyed look; Mort because he liked the spirit of a man that was proud to wear his Union army tunic when the Texans were riding high in Abilene. Like the mayor he came quickly to the same conclusion that m'be with a little more incentive, like more pay for the job, the big stranger could be won over to wearing a peace officer's star. He looked man enough to have the balls to make the trail-hands respect the law in Abilene.

Julie's heart was fluttering most un-whore like. It had been a long time since she had seen such a walking-tall, clean-cut featured man. She sighed. He'd sure make a welcome change to the bow-legged, cowshit-smelling Texans. Julie shivered; or that fat pig, Tod, scaring her with what he'd do to her with his big knife. Why, she thought, cheering herself up, if a girl hadn't to earn her living she'd take the big man upstairs for free. But business was business so she got back to her task of trying to get the tight-fisted drummer to part with two dollars in exchange for a short-time romp upstairs.

Mort moved to serve his new customer and Frank thought as he came up to the bar that the time was ripe for him to put on his act again for the benefit of Mort Dunstan. He couldn't see the two tipsy trail-hands giving him any trouble if they took offence at his running them down. If the bar had been full of Texans then he would have heeded Phil's warning, and his own common sense, and made his anti-reb feelings known to more sympathetic ears. Frank gave Mort a lip-curling, beady-eyed look of disdain as the bar owner placed a glass and a bottle of whiskey in front of him. He jerked a thumb at Phil and the two trail-hands.

'Do you clean out this rat-trap every time those reb trash leave after they've been drinking here, mister?' Frank stepped closer to Phil and jabbed him aggressively on the shoulder. 'I bumped into you on the street just now, bub. We had words and I warned you then to keep out from under my feet, remember? I'm warning you again, if you so much as block the sunlight from me I might just forget that you've only got one wing.' Frank turned and stared down the two trail-hands. 'And that goes for you two ugly-faced saddle-tramps as well.'

The two "bums" hurriedly drank off their whiskies and made for the door, casting over-the-shoulder nervous glances at the big hard-nosed blue-belly. Phil, with a show of righteous anger on his face, said before he followed the two out, 'You'll not be so loud-mouthed when the rest of the boys ride into town, you Yankee bastard!'

Frank gave him a sneering, stomping man's grin of contempt and turned back and faced Mort. Mort wasn't happy for his saloon to be called a rat-trap; it was no better than the Texans expected, but he wasn't about to disagree with a gift horse. Thinking along the same lines as the mayor again the boy would have to tone down his attitude towards the trail-hands or he wouldn't last long as sheriff. It was as the crippled kid said, a whole army of them would descend on the town and jump on him but hard. The boy had the right feeling towards the Texans, the same as his. He would make a first-class lawman, bringing Yankee law and order to Abilene. He removed the bottle of whiskey from the bar top and brought up another one from below the bar, his own special whiskey

'Drinks on the house, stranger.' He smiled. 'I'm Mort Dunstan, owner of this rat-trap. Are you staying long in town?'

'Could be, Mr Dunstan,' replied Frank.

Mort hoped it would be long enough for him to twist the mayor's arm into making the kid sheriff. He nodded his head slightly at Julie. Julie, all smiles got up from the drummer's table and came up to the bar and slipped her hand through Frank's.

'My name is Julie,' she said. 'Care if I join you, big fella?'

NINE

Newly appointed town sheriff Frank Eberhart, an extra pistol jutting up above the top of his pants, and a double-barrelled shotgun cradled in his arms, was doing his first nightly rounds of the saloons and bawdy houses.

After serving him a drink and telling him to help himself Mort had left the saloon, leaving him in the more than friendly hands of Julie, which put Frank in something of a moral dilemma.

Although he had been brought up in a strict Lutheran religious household where sex outside the bounds of holy wedlock was a mortal sin, Frank had enjoyed his fair share of women of the night. A man who knew he was liable to be tapped on the shoulder by the Grim Reaper and called to account by way of a reb shell or bullet, was entitled to indulge in at least one of the sins of the flesh. A week or so ago he would have enjoyed taking the sweet-smiling redhead upstairs. Since meeting Mrs Farrow he felt that it would not be right and proper to seek the services of a pretty young whore. And he wondered why.

He had no claim on Mrs Farrow and she had none on him. Yet the way he felt about her, going with a saloon girl would sully those thoughts. That

she would never know and if she ever did wouldn't
give a damn what her cook did in his own time
didn't help Frank to sort out his mixed-up
reasoning. One thing was for sure, what had
started out as a journey to help an unknown
widow-woman was turning out a lot more
complicated than he could have even dreamed of.
Frank was trying hard to come up with some
excuse to decline Julie's invitation without
offending her, making her think that he was too
high and mighty to go upstairs with a common
saloon girl. The three men that came into the
saloon resolved that problem for him.

The three wore range-working garb and had
heavy calibre pistols belted about their bellies;
stone-faced, watchful-eyed individuals. Too
uptight Frank thought to be trail-hands coming in
to paint the town red. The trio gave him an
unblinking-eyed lookover and what they saw in
him didn't register any change on two of the mens'
faces. The fat man's face showed real anger and
Frank was beginning to think that m'be the men
were Texans and his Union army jacket was
upsetting the fat man, till he heard Julie gasp, 'Oh
hell, Tod;' withdrawing her arm from his, and
realised that the fat man was directing his anger at
the girl.

The three crossed over to a table set back in an
alcove, the barkeep hurrying after them with a
bottle of whiskey and three glasses on a tray.
Before he sat down the fat man, Tod, called out,
'Get yourself over here, Red, pronto. It's my
money that's buyin' you!'

Julie made a twisted mirthless face at Frank and
left him to join the three at the table. Tod grabbed

her and pulled her roughly down on to his knees.
His face suddenly twisted in pain. 'Watch where
you put your arm, you bitch!' he angrily snarled.
'I've got a busted shoulder.'

Frank stiffened up at the bar, nerve ends
jumping. Could he have got lucky so quick he
thought. As casually as his excitement would let
him he gave the fat man a closer look. He didn't
recognize him as being one of the raiders but it had
been dark, fast-moving action, not the ideal
situation for him to have obtained a good
description of any of the gang. Yet he knew for
sure that he had wounded one of them in the right
shoulder, the same shoulder that the man Julie
named as Tod was holding as he cursed the
ashen-faced girl for her clumsiness.

Frank was well aware that Tod could have
injured his shoulder other than being hit by a
Winchester shell in the middle of a dark night
during a raid. He could have fallen off his horse,
fallen down when drunk, but his instincts wouldn't
let him buy that bill of sale. The three of them he
saw now had the stamp of hard men, taking men,
eyes forever flickering towards the door, sitting
with their backs against a wall; men who even in the
quietness of the saloon couldn't completely relax,
lower their guards.

Tod had the cold-eyed, merciless stare of a
hurting man, a killing man, if the mood took him.
Julie was still sitting on his knee being pawed and
by the fixed frightened grimace on her face Frank
opined that he had summed up Tod right. That
reading of the fat man left Frank in no doubt,
ignoring the odds against finding any signs of
Captain Hardin and his gang in so short a time,

that he was facing three of the captain's men. There was one other thing that set Frank's brain ticking, the three men were drinking Mr Dunstan's best whiskey. So there must be a special relationship between the saloon owner and the marauders.

Frank drank off his whiskey. He had to contact Phil and get him to follow the three men when they left the saloon. He would stay close by, keep an eye on Mort Dunstan and when he got the chance, ask Julie about Tod, unsuspicious like. She could also be linked with the gang somehow; Tod certainly had a hold on her. He could see by her face that the fat man was anything but her beau but when Tod called her she went running to him.

The best place to do the questioning was in her room upstairs after a bed-bouncing session with her. Mrs Farrow's life was worth lowering his moral principles. Before Frank could put his rapidly thought up plan into action, such as it was, Mort, accompanied by the mayor came bustling into the saloon.

'Ah, Mr Eberhart,' the mayor greeted him, his smile stretching right up to his ears. 'I'm glad you're still here. That job I mentioned that I might be able to fix you up with, well, Mr Eberhart, Mr Dunstan here thinks that I should offer it to you right now without waiting for the go ahead from Deputy Marshal Calder. As Mayor of the town I think that it's within my power to do the choosing myself.' The mayor switched off his just-one-the-boys smile and put on his official business look, as stern and resolute as his paunchy face allowed his muscles to tighten up. Frank was beginning to think that the pair of them were putting him

forward as a candidate for State Governor when
the mayor finally came to the point and said. 'I
would like to offer you the town sheriff's post, Mr
Eberhart.' His big smile came back as held out his
open hand. Frank saw the sheen of a peace officer's
star resting on the palm of it. 'If you'd care to
accompany me to my office we can discuss the finer
points of a sheriff's duty.'

And here he was, making his first patrol as
sheriff, Frank thought. the fastest appointment
and acceptance of the post of peace officer in the
history of Abilene. Yet he hadn't blindly unthink-
ingly succumbed to the high pressure sales talk
from the mayor and Mort Dunstan. He had quickly
weighed up the pros and cons of wearing the
badge. On the plus side he could walk in and out of
the Texas Drover, keeping tabs on Tod and his
buddies, or anyone else that warranted a closer
look, without raising any suspicious hackles, and
keep in Mort Dunstan's good books by curbing the
wilder excesses of the trail-hands drinking at his
bar, win his confidence then m'be one day he might
just let slip how he was tied in with Captain
Hardin's raiders. Then there was what Julie knew
about Tod. Three possible leads to check out
regarding the whereabouts of Captain Hardin; a
better than ever chance of succeeding in what had
only been a wild idea back in Texas.

Of course he had to stay alive to be able to do all
this nosing around for what came with the badge
was the risk of getting plugged by any Texan,
drunk or sober, that fancied a Yankee sheriff's
scalp hanging on his belt. He wouldn't have to
sound off at them at all to prove that he was a
genuine reb-hater. The tin star, and its law, to men

whose only understanding of the law was what a
Colt or a Winchester dished out, could bring him
all the grief he could handle. But he was a big man
and he carried a big gun. And Phil was watching
his back. Or would be when he contacted him and
told him about the men in the saloon, and that he
wore a peace officer's badge.

Crossing the black opening of a side alley
alongside some boarded-up lots Frank suddenly
heard the sound of running footsteps. He whirled
round on his heels to face the danger but before he
could make a move to defend himself, with fist or
gun, they were on him, raining blows at him. It was
too dark and he was too hard pressed to spare the
time to count the exact number of assailants who
had sprung at him from out of the darkness of the
alley.

A savage blow to his kidneys brought tears to his
eyes, making him gasp out in pain, causing him to
drop the shotgun as he staggered forward, head on
to a bony knuckled fist that set bells ringing loudly
in his ears. He lashed out wildly with his right hand
and felt it contact with one of his attackers' faces
that drew a cry of pain from him. Then he sank to
his knees, sobbing in agony, as a swinging foot
caught him low down, fortunately for Frank not at
full strength, or the fight would have been over
there and then.

With the acid taste of bile clawing at the back of
his throat Frank, mad-eyed with pain and rage,
somehow summoned up the last reserves of his
great strength. Shaking his head like a big shaggy
buffalo to clear his vision, ignoring the fearful
burning at his crotch, he straightened up, arms
outflung, bellowing like the same buffalo he

brushed his attackers back from him. It was only a brief respite as the men closed in on him again but it gave Frank time enough to make a grab for the pistol in his pants top while with his left arm he tried to protect himself from the worst of the blows. He could feel no comforting butt, it must have fallen out during the struggle. Frantically his hand dove for his holstered pistol. Black despair swept over him like a sickness when his scrabbling fingers found only an empty holster. The pistol, he fleetingly thought had been taken by the men who were beating him up.

Frank then really did go mad. Kicking, arm-swinging, yelling, he charged at the ring of men hoping to break through and run like hell for the nearest brightly lit saloon, to make a final stand where he could see the men who were attacking him. Through the blood hammering in his ears Frank heard the sickening thud of something solid striking something soft and a shadow fell away from in front of him. Dimly he heard another thuck of a man being pistol whipped. This time one of the attackers yelled in pain as he dropped to the ground. Then came an alarmed shout from one of them of, 'Let's get to hell outa it! The big sonuvabitch has got help!' Just as suddenly as they had come Frank's assailants melted back into the blackness of the alley, leaving Frank swaying on his feet like the town drunk, with his balls burning like live embers and his back feeling as though it had been pierced by an Indian's lance. The pain in his face and ribs he could live with.

'Are you OK?' said an anxious-sounding Phil, putting out his good arm to steady Frank.

'Yeah,' Frank gasped out painfully. 'I think so.

But if you asked me that question after another coupla minutes more tangling with those fellas I reckon I would have had to say no I ain't. I think they had me beat. Thanks for butting in.'

'It's what you should've expected, Frank. Those two trail-hands you rousted put it around that there was a hard-nosed Yankee in town spitting smoke and fire against Texans. Some of the boys took it in their heads to come riding into town to cut you down to size. You're lucky they only intended beating you up. A trail-hand that fancied himself a *pistolero* could have been with them.'

'The way I'm feeling right now,' Frank said. 'I'd welcome a bullet in the brain with the greatest of pleasure. I'll not upset the Texans any more, well no more than I have to do as Sheriff of Abilene. Nothing personal you understand, just in the line of duty.'

Phil let out his breath in one long disbelieving whistle. 'Jee-sus,' he said. 'Ain't you got enough on your plate tryin' to capture Captain Hardin and all his gang without taking on the job as town sheriff? This is a wide-open town during the trailin' season, Frank. Only lame-brained *hombres* that's fed up with livin' take to wearing a lawman's badge in a trail-end town.'

'It won't be for long, Phil,' Frank said. And he told him about the men in the saloon and the tie-up he felt there was between them and Captain Hardin, plus the possible involvement of Mort Dunstan in the whole scheme of things. He gave Phil a painful grin. 'Besides, you'll be watching my back, sorta my unofficial deputy. But don't hang back so long next time. And I swear to Holy God I won't prod the Texans any more. Now I must get back to my office and get cleaned up and earn my due. Mort Dunstan will be worrying when the new sheriff will be showing up. It was him that wanted one; feared in case the Texans burnt his saloon down. If the fat man or his two buddies are in the saloon I'll give you the nod. Then you can practise your tracking skills and find out where they hole-up. Can't be too far from town.'

'Does that mean I'll get a deputy's badge, Mr Eberhart?' said Phil, innocently.

Frank laughed then groaned loudly. 'You'll get my boot up your ass, boy, if you don't help me to find my two pistols. It kinda hurts me to bend right now.'

'Sure thing, Yankee,' said Phil.'But what about these two here?' Phil jabbed his toe into one of the men he had laid his gun barrel on.

'Leave 'em,' replied Frank. 'The way I'm feeling I'll hardly get myself back to my office. I'd never lug them there.'

'OK,' said Phil. 'I'll see you around then.'

There was a small disturbance taking place in the Texas Drover saloon when Frank strode into the bar, walking tall, with great difficulty, shotgun cradled in his arms. Face twisted in a savage grimace, more with the pain he was suffering than the hard-man's image he was trying to put over, in reality all Frank wanted to do was to crawl into his bunk and pass out. The scuffle between some poker players was being dealt with by Mort's bouncers and Frank stood aside as two trail-hands, shouting and struggling, were run out of the saloon by three heavily-built men and thrown bodily into the street.

Mort smiled at him and waved for him to come
over to the bar. Mr Eberhart, he thought, looked
like a real peace officer. By the fierce thrust of his
jaw ready to cut loose with his shotgun to prevent
the Texan assholes from wrecking his place. He
was glad that the boy had not taken to wearing his
uniform on his rounds. Realizing that a man who
had faced Lee's army wearing that tunic with pride
wouldn't want to shed it when confronted by a
bunch of Texans, he had as diplomatically as
possible, told him that there was no need to seek
out extra trouble. No need to wave a red flag at the
bull.

'Have a drink, Sheriff,' Mort said when Frank
bellied up to the bar.

'No thanks, Mr Dunstan.' Frank smiled a
country-boy-like guileless grin. 'I don't reckon that
the mayor would take kindly to me drinking on
duty.' *And he'd take less kindly to you if I can
prove that you're tied in with Captain Hardin and
his gang.* Frank thought grimly.

'As you wish, Sheriff,' said Mort. 'If you change
your mind and I'm not about just ask the barkeep
for the special bottle.' He smiled at Frank. 'It's the
best blue-belly brand, too good for those rebs to
pour down their dirty throats.'

At that surprising remark from a man who made
his living off Texans, Frank tallied Mort Dunstan
as another man still fighting the war. Making his
connections with Captain Hardin, another man
who strongly believed that General Grant should
never had made peace with the South, all that more
certain.

Before leaving Frank cast a look at the table in
the alcove. The fat man and the man whom he had

been with weren't sitting there but what did catch his interest, made him think more than ever that he was following a hot trail, was that the two men at the table now were of the same hard-faced type. Men, in Frank's considered opinion who earned their living by killing men and stealing their cattle. Frank inclined his head at Phil who was standing at the bar and pointed with his chin at the men in the corner. On seeing Phil's head turn in their direction he strolled casually out of the saloon.

It was an old man of ninety, aching in every joint, who limped back to the sheriff's office. Heeling off his boots and unbuckling his gunbelt Frank lowered himself slowly down on to the bunk. Covering his face with his hat he closed his eyes and dropped off into a dreamless sleep, Mrs Farrow, the Double Star herd, Captain Hardin forgotten as he lay silent and unmoving as one dead.

TEN

Captain Hardin was a long ways from sleep, deep and peaceful, or otherwise. He was pacing to and fro along the porch of Mort Dunstan's ranch-house chewing savagely on a cigar whose business end had long since died out with neglect, worried about the way events were building up against him. The loss of five of his men gave him cause for concern. All of them knew that they were living on borrowed time. Some day a Union cavalry troop or a marshal's posse would catch up with them. They were dead men in all but fact. But men lost on an abortive raid was too big a loss for his small band to take.

He had led his men like some greenhorn shavetail into a goddamned ambush. If it hadn't been then he was losing his luck riding into another bunch of men in the middle of nowhere. And when a man's luck deserts him it's time for some soul-searching, or he would soon have no men left to lead. They'd been lucky to come through that mistake with only five men lost. He couldn't afford to make another one.

M'be his luck would return if he operated in new territory; raid the herds between the Red and the Brazos; catch the Texans wrong-footed on their

own piece of prairie. He had heard that some of
William C Quantrill's old gang of secessionists had
taken up raiding Union banks in Kansas and as far
north as Minnesota. In the morning he would
discuss with Sergeant Kegg whether they should go
into the bank-raiding business. Southern banks. A
bank in some quiet dog-shit Texas town that would
raise no sweat removing the money from its
strongroom.

Bad luck or not riding alongside him, Captain
Hardin was not about to surrender or go crawling
in asking for amnesty for him and his men from
the sons-of-bitches that decided the war was over.
As long as he had breath in his body and brave men
that would follow him he would continue the
struggle against the enemy, the Texans.

The captain's hatred for the South and what it
stood for, the continuation of slavery, hadn't come
about by a single traumatic happening that had
turned Mort Dunstan overnight into a convert and
fervent supporter of the Union cause. The captain
had been born and raised in an anti-slavery family.
He had ridden as a young man with John Brown
the Abolitionist when they raided the pro-slavery
settlement at Pottawatomie Creek. His father, a
brother, two cousins and several other kin had paid
the full price in the small battles waged between
them and the Border Ruffians. Small maybe in
their size but big, fierce in their blood-letting.

The captain clamped his jaws vice-like on his
cigar. No sir, he angrily thought, he would never
stomach ass-kissing General Robert E Lee and
calling him friend. He stopped chewing at the cigar
and spat out the butt and turned and went back
inside the house. M'be he could sleep now that he

had sorted things out a little. Sergeant Kegg was inside waiting to report to him.

'Two of the men, Jud and Elliot, are due in at any time, Captain,' he said. 'Tod's staying the night in Abilene and the night guard has been posted.'

'Good,' replied Captain Hardin. He liked to keep tabs on his men. They could never know when they would have to move out fast. 'You can stand down for the night now, Sergeant, but come to my quarters after breakfast. I've got some ideas of how we should operate in the future. I'd like to go over them with you before we put them to the men. Till tomorrow then, and good night, Sergeant.'

Phil had worked with longhorns all his life and knew from that experience that the two men Frank had pointed out to him weren't trail-hands, didn't hail from Texas either. They had the mean-faced looks of a couple of bad-asses. He followed them out of the saloon and waited till they had got on horses before he got astride his and began to tail them.

Phil couldn't see the men he was trailing but followed them by the sound of the half-drunken ribaldry that passed between them. He calculated that he must have ridden seven, eight miles from Abilene. He couldn't tell for sure as the pair kept stopping to empty their bladders. He was beginning to think that it could be an all night trail when he saw a lamp-lit building break the darkness in the far distance. Suddenly he heard one of the men ahead yell out, 'It's us, Ned! Me and Elliott, we're comin' on in!'

An 'OK' was shouted back in reply from somewhere in the thick timber at the left of the trail. Exactly where in the blackness of the night Phil couldn't exactly pinpoint. The "OK" was followed by, 'Did you get to hump that redhead, Jud?'

Phil heard Jud give a coarse laugh. 'You know that gal is Tod's personal property when he's in town. No two-dollar whore however purty she looks ain't worth being worked over by Tod with that big pig-sticker he totes around. See you at chow, Ned. Let's go, Elliott, before I've got to step down and take another piss. I'm fair worn out climbing back on.'

Phil heard the sounds of their voices fading away into the night. He'd found out where the men laid their heads down, to press on any further was risking being heard by the unseen lookout. His being on the trail only confirmed what, like Frank, he had suspected when he first saw the men. A normal run ranch with a regular crew had no reason to post a lookout on a main trail. But men with law-breaking habits wouldn't be able to rest easy at nights unless they had a man watching their back-trail.

He would have a word with Frank in the morning about his conclusions and if he thought it wise he would come this way in daylight for a proper scout. Phil pulled round his mount to head back to Abilene. The horse had only taken a few steps when it slipped on the lip of a gully, kicking down a slither of dirt and stones into its depths in its panic to regain its footing, the rattling noise breaking the silence of the night. And Phil painfully found the exact location of the lookout.

He saw a gun flash away to his right and felt a hammerlike blow at his left shoulder that brought back fearful memories. One thing did give Phil some comfort, the bastard's lucky shot had only torn a lump more off his already chewed-up left arm. Gritting his teeth with pain he fought the natural self-preservation urge to rib-kick his horse into a get-the-hell-out-of-it gallop. The noise that would make could draw another shot from the lookout and tell him that someone was snooping around out here. Before he knew it a whole pack of them could be hunting him down. Keeping low down, Indian fashion, on his horse Phil let it have its head, praying that it wouldn't clumsy-foot its way into another gulley.

Jud and Elliott swung their ponies round and raced back along the trail, sobered up enough to have fisted their pistols, and dragged them to a dirt-raising halt at Ned's hideout.

'Trouble?' Jud curtly asked.

'Thought it was, Jud,' Ned answered. 'Heard something; could have been just a critter of sorts, winged a shot in its direction. Ain't heard nothin' since. Could have scared it away.'

'You musta been imaginin' it, Ned,' Jud said. 'Thinking about that redhead at Mort's has put your nerves on edge. Mine are all shot to hell just thinking of what fat Tod could be doing to her right now.'

'M'be so,' growled Ned. 'But I did hear something and it don't pay to take chances. Better report it to the sergeant when you get back. See what he thinks. You know how that captain wants to know everything that's goin' on.'

'Yeah, I'll do just that,' promised Jud. But he thought that the sergeant would think that Ned's nerves had played him wrong.

Sergeant Kegg opined just that and didn't think that it was important enough for him to wake up the captain. Not that he completely ignored Jud's report. It was better to be safe than sorry especially when sorry could mean dead. So before he settled down for the night he doubled the prowler guard around the perimeter of the ranch. They knew their orders, shoot at anything they saw moving and ask the "why fors" later.

Well out of rifle range Phil stopped his horse and pulled off his bandanna then with teeth and good arm he managed to wrap it round his wound. As far as he could judge it was only a flesh wound, just below his shoulder. The arm bandaged to his satisfaction, he gave his horse a sharp dig in the ribs and rode back to Abilene at a steady canter, convinced that he had done a good couple of hours' work.

ELEVEN

Frank gingerly levered himself up from his bunk. His restful sleep had eased some of the pain the Texans had inflicted on him but he was still as stiff in the joints as an old man. He examined his upper body through his shaving mirror. His right side, the side that had caught the brunt of the kicking, was a mass of greenish bruises. One side of his face caused a little pain when he opened and shut his mouth, but as far as he could feel he had suffered no broken bones and although tender down at his groin his manhood had not been impaired.

He had known from the start that he hadn't much time to find out where Captain Hardin and his gang were holed-up. Last night he found out the hard way that time was shorter than he had thought. Another attack by riled Texans could mean that he had no time left at all. He'd be in hospital or planted on Boot Hill. He would have to try and speed things up. Instead of creeping around with ears cocked, listening for any gossip about the marauders, direct questions would have to be asked. The redhead, Julie, would do to begin with. She was closely acquainted, m'be not by mutual desire Frank conceded, with the fat man, Tod, his number one suspect for being a member of Captain Hardin's gang. It would probably blow his cover wide open but it was a calculated risk. First he had to see Phil to find out how he fared last night. As it was, it was Phil who sought him out.

Frank was locking the door of his office prior to setting off to do his tour of the town when Phil hailed him from further along the street.

'Hold on there, sheriff, I've a complaint to make! About the way you're allowing drunks to shoot off their hoglegs in town. Some asshole put a slug in my arm last night. Ain't there no law against that sort of foolhardy behaviour?' Phil had shouted loud enough for the early morning citizens of the town going about their lawful business to hear every word. Phil was no John Wilkes Booth but he knew how to play a role. He had to if he and Frank didn't want to end up dead.

'There sure is, mister,' replied Frank. 'If you'd care to step into my office and file an official complaint ...' He unlocked the door and led Phil inside.

Phil's pale, drawn, sunken-eyed face and the dark bloodstained bandage on his upper arm took the colour out of his own face. His decision to get things moving had been the right one or they could both end up dead. 'Christ, Phil!' he gasped. 'What sorta trouble did you ride into last night?'

Phil gave him a lopsided boyish grin of success at a job well done. 'No trouble, Frank,' he said. 'Just a slight accident. But if my thinkin's right the slug I took was fired by one of Captain Hardin's boys acting as a lookout. Kinda proves what you felt the first time you saw those fellas sitting drinking in the saloon.' Then he told Frank where he had trailed the men to.

'Good work, Phil,' Frank said. 'I think we've hit the jackpot. It must be a ranch of sorts they've holed-up in. The gang comes into Abilene in their twos and threes for their pleasures like regular ranch-hands. It's a perfect setup. The army and marshal's posses are running all over Kansas like headless chickens trying to seek the bastards out and there they are, a coupla arrow shots away from where we're standing. There's still one snag, Phil, we haven't got proof that they are who we know they are. I've never seen any likeness of the gang so I can't ask for a marshal's posse to be raised on suspicion alone.'

'I was thinkin' that m'be I could round up some of the boys,' said Phil eagerly. Then not so hopefully he added. 'But it would be no good for the crazy sonsuvbitches would go charging out of town hootin' and a'hollerin' as though were back in General Hood's division trying to take the Union cannon on Cemetery Ridge way up at Gettysburg, frightening Captain Hardin and his boys away before they got near enough to have a shot at them.'

'What we've got to do,' Frank said, 'must be fast and quiet, or watch and wait. We're dealing with cagey men. The first hint of danger it will be as you say, Phil, they'll be long gone.'

'We've got to do something, Frank,' pleaded Phil. 'Don't tell me I got myself shot for damn all!'

'You didn't, Phil. We go and ask that redhead in Mort's saloon a few questions. She'll know something about the men that use her. How many of them there are. That at least will give us a clearer picture of what we're up against.' Frank grinned. 'As if we don't already know. If she can't or won't tell us anything there's always Mort. I reckon he's involved with the gang somehow.'

'There's another fella you can ask,' Phil said. 'One of the men I was trailin' mentioned to the lookout that Tod was stayin' in town. Got the hots for the redhead you're after questioning he said.'

'I know about his liking of the redhead, Phil,' replied Frank. 'Tod's the guy with the hurt shoulder. I've a gut feeling I gave it to him during the raid on Luke Dolan's cattle. So I think that we'll stay well clear of asking him any questions. He'd shoot us down like dogs before we even opened our mouths, or warn the captain that someone is sniffing around for information about the raiders. If we don't get any joy from the girl or Mort we'll ride out to the ranch and keep an eye on the place till the captain makes his next move. M'be we'll get lucky, catch the bastards unawares again, shoot some of them down without hurt to ourselves.' Frank gave Phil's wound a concerned look. 'You get that arm fixed by a regular sawbones first, Phil, then we'll work as before. 'I'll do the open part,you stay close and loose as a back-up.' Frank smiled. 'Next time I need help I'll holler real loud, you can bet on it.'

TWELVE

Julie, sitting on her bed, pulled her wrap tighter about her. She struck a match but her hand shook so much that the flame went out before she could light up the thin cigarillo that dangled loosely in her mouth. 'Damnit!' she said and flung the cigarillo to the floor. She couldn't stand another session with that fat slob, Tod. Not even if he paid her his weight in gold. The way he played around with that big knife after he had used her scared the hell out of her. The mad-assed son-of-a-bitch threatened to cut her up some so that she wouldn't be able to entertain no more. Last night, what with the pain of his wound and all, he acted real loco. Julie opened her robe and gazed again at the angry red weals across the creamy whiteness of her stomach, Tod's drunken handiwork with his knife.

Julie burst into tears. She tried lighting another cigarillo. This time she succeeded and as she drew the calming smoke down into her lungs her nerves steadied somewhat. 'Damnit!' she said out aloud again. Then decided that as soon as the pig left that saloon she'd pack her bags and catch the next eastbound train leaving the depot. Get herself a job in a decent cathouse in a decent town, where men had manners and knew how to treat a girl. A whore's life in a trail-end town of bad liquor and rough men was sure no bed of roses. That greasy-bellied bastard, Tod, made it a bed of thorns.

Julie got up from her bed and idly glanced out of the window. She saw the clean cut Yankee she'd briefly chatted up before the mayor dragged him away to pin a sheriff's star on his shirt. The big greenhorn didn't know it but he had as good as signed his own death warrant. The Texans when liquored up would crucify him. In spite of her disparaging thoughts about Abilene men in general and of Tod in particular, Julie felt her sap rise at the sight of the new sheriff.

Now there was a man she just knew would know how to treat a girl, she thought. He was talking to the young crippled Texan kid, the one he had almost slung out of the saloon. She couldn't hear what they were saying but she saw them both smile real friendly-like before parting. The kid crossing the street to Mayor Bailey's store, the big Yankee coming towards the saloon. Julie gasped excitedly and threw off her wrap and hastily began to dress herself before fixing up her face. M'be, if Tod got to hell out of town after he'd eaten, she could carry on where she'd left off with the new sheriff. Julie giggled. That's if town sheriffs were allowed to hump on duty. Then another thought struck her. Why were the kid and him so friendly now? Julie quickly stopped thinking why. If she tried to fathom out the devious and lowdown traits and habits of all the men that she had shared her bed with she would have no time to think of anything else.

Frank entered the Texas Drover by the back

entrance. His questioning of Julie was something he didn't want Mort Dunstan to know about. A barkeep was filling crates with empty whiskey bottles by the door and Frank asked him if Mort was up and about. The barkeep favoured Frank with a bleery-eyed look.

'You must be kiddin', Sheriff,' he said. 'He don't come down till the sun lifts above the Church Meeting House roof.'

'How about the redhead, Julie?' Frank then asked. 'Is she out of bed?'

The barkeep's eyes widened and brightened with surprise. He knew men that couldn't face another day without a slug of redeye but this early for bouncing Julie just to set a man right? Then again he charitably thought that when the Texans rode in for their regular night's carousing the sheriff would be hard pressed to find time to break wind.

'She's up I guess,' he said. 'Her boyfriend is in the back, eatin'. She's in room four, upstairs and to your left, Sheriff.'

'Thanks,' replied Frank. As he made to go to the barkeep caught hold of his aim.

'I don't like putting a damper on a man having his pleasure, Sheriff,' he said, 'and I sure hope that you don't mind me telling you, but don't spend too long upstairs. That fella Tod is not the most sociable of characters. In fact he ain't sociable at all and the sonuvabitch is an expert with a knife.'

'Thanks again,' said Frank. 'I don't intend staying long and no offence taken. A man would be downright foolish not to heed a warning.'

Julie heard a kock on her door and all her fears came flooding back till she realized that it couldn't be Tod as he hadn't the manners to knock on a girl's door before entering. She took a quick but professional look at herself in the mirror and walked across the room and opened the door.

'Why what a pleasant surprise, Sheriff,' she said. Her smile was warm and genuine, anything but professional. Tod and his threats were a million miles away. 'But it's a little early,' she waved an arm vaguely behind her. 'The room's in a bit of a mess.'

Frank grinned. 'It's a business call, business for me that is, not pleasure, unfortunately. May I step inside, Miss Julie?'

Trying not to show her disappointment in spite of knowing that she was crazy to think that it was remotely possible for her to have fun and games with the big desirable Yankee when Tod was only a floorboard's thickness away, she stepped aside. 'Why certainly, Sheriff.' Reaching down Julie swept up a heap of soiled clothes from a chair and flung them on the unmade bed. 'Please sit down.'

Her smile was a little forced, fearful now of Tod's reaction if he came up and found her with another man, however innocent it might be. In spite of her worries Julie felt that the big Yankee was man enough to protect her, stop Tod from hurting her. And the big man did wear a peace officer's badge. That also could have a calming effect on Tod, till he returned tonight that is, for he never forgot a slight. Julie's smile vanished altogether. But what the hell, she thought, a few minutes with a real polite-looking man like the sheriff was worth the risk of what Tod might do to her. Besides this time tonight she would be sitting in a railcar miles away from Tod.

Frank took off his hat and sat down, angling the chair round till it part-faced the door. He didn't need the barkeep's warning about Tod's mean disposition. The marauders weren't noted for their drawing-room manners. Julie, in spite of her fears, sat on the edge of her bed, bright-eyed, hands clasped across her lap. Just because she was a whore in a dog-shit trail-town, she thought, servicing drunken, dirty-mouthing Texans, it didn't mean that she couldn't act like a real lady when a man paid a visit to her as though he had come to partake tea with her; didn't mean that she couldn't show a little class when the occasion required it. She raised a questioning eyebrow. 'Well, Sheriff?' she asked softly.

Frank came straight to the point. Tod could come barging in at any moment.

'This fella, Tod, you're friendly with,' he said, 'how much do you know about him, Miss Julie? What does he do for a living? Do you know anything about the men that come into town with him?'

Julie's back stiffened in anger, her face stoned over. Her soft maidenly look switched into a whore's hard professional face. Ready, as one of her calling had to be, it came with the trade, for any physical blow or verbal insult aimed at her with seemingly unfeeling toughness. 'That asshole isn't any friend of mine, Sheriff,' she snapped angrily. 'Believe me I wouldn't have the fat slob as a client for all the gold in Califoni', I have to put up with him because if I don't he'll cut me up with that big knife he carries around. Why ... why I could show you ...' Julie burst into tears. 'Friend!' I wish the bastard would drop dead,' she sobbed bitterly.

'I'm sorry I upset you, Miss Julie,' Frank said, embarrassedly, 'I had to ask; it's important, people's lives may depend on me finding out all I can about Tod. I know all about scum like him but he won't hurt you none, Miss Julie, and that's a fact.' He smiled. 'And call me Frank. I'm not used to being called Sheriff.'

Julie smiled wanly back at him through her tears, reassured by his quiet matter-of-fact promise, knowing deep inside her that it wasn't a blowhard's idle boast. 'OK, Frank,' she said. 'Keep asking, I'll help if I can.'

'Did he mention a Captain Hardin?' questioned Frank. 'This ranch he stays on, do you know who the owner is?'

'I've never heard Tod mention a Captain Hardin, Frank,' replied Julie. 'But he's real tight-lipped. Only opens his mouth to eat or drink, or yell at me. He belongs to a bunch that come in regularly from the Cross L ranch, just west of here. All mean-faced hombres but not so mean as Tod.' Julie gave Frank a real smile again. 'A working girl don't have the time or the inclination to write out case histories like some doc on all her clients. But I tell you this, Frank, for what it's worth, they don't horse around like ranch-hands and they've got more cash to throw around than any honest, hard-working cowboy could earn in a long time. As for who owns the Cross L, well, you should be talking to Mort about that, because he's the man that occupies the big house there when he's not staying in town.'

Frank felt an inner feeling of satisfaction. He had made more progress than he could have ever expected; found out where the gang was, discovered the name of the man that was fronting for them, and pinpointed some of the gang. Then came the hard bit, how to rope them all in before they rode out on their next raid.

'Mort was next on my list for questioning, Julie,' Frank told her. 'I suspected that he was involved with the gang in some way. By what you've told me I can squeeze him real hard to spill all he knows about the men he has on his ranch passing themselves off as ranch-hands.'

'Don't have anything to do with Tod, Frank,' Julie warned. 'Unless you've got some deputies to back you up.' She got up from the bed and rested her hands on Frank's shoulders. Serious-faced she said, 'Tod's a hair-trigger man at the best of times. Right now isn't a good time for him. He took a slug in his shoulder, he hasn't told me who from, but it's hurting him bad. But not bad enough, it should have killed him,' Julie added venomously.

Frank smiled at her. 'I was trying to do just that when I cut loose at him, Julie. Next time I get him in my sights I hope to rectify that mistake.'

Julie gasped in slack-jawed amazement. 'Why you big hellion,' she breathed. 'You've made my day.' Putting her arms around Frank's neck she bent lower and kissed him full on the lips. She still had her arms about Frank when Tod kicked open the door and burst into the room.

With a vicious swing of his left arm Tod caught Julie a blow on the side of her head that flung her backwards across the bed with a sharp cry of pain, half-dazed and tasting the saltiness of blood in her mouth. Tod's right hand jabbed the knife point under Frank's chin, stiffening him into a rigid-backed, head-held-high stance as he eye-balled Tod. It was a big knife and Frank didn't doubt that Tod had honed it to razor sharpness.

His busted shoulder didn't seem to present any difficulty for him in using it. Frank was sitting here looking at death as close as he had gazed on the Grim Reaper during the war. What churned him up almost as much as having the knife at his throat was that he had promised Julie that Tod wouldn't get the chance of harming her again, the big fast-thinking Yankee would protect her. Some promise, he bitterly thought.

'Look at me the wrong way, you big sonuvabitch,' Tod snarled, 'and I'm goin' to make a hell of a mess on this randy bitch's carpet. That bit of tin on your chest don't cut any ice with me. Now you just tell me why you've been chattin' to the redhead. I heard you both rabbitin' on outside in the hall.'

Julie raised herself shakily up from the bed. 'He was only trying to fix up a session with me, Tod, that's all. I was just telling him I wasn't available.'

'Shut your lyin' mouth,' Tod spat at her, without taking his eyes off Frank. 'You were all over the sonuvabitch when I came in. I'll deal with you later. Now, Mister Sheriff, you just tell me why you came snoopin' up here to talk to that whore or I'll start cuttin'.'

Julie, in a cold unpanicky anger, rapidly weighed up her chances of getting out of the perilous situation she was in. There was a slight possibility, she couldn't put it any higher than that, if she could distract Tod's attention for a second or two it might give Frank his chance to make a fight of it. It wasn't just selfishness on her part that was making her think that way though she knew that if Frank was killed she could kiss goodbye forever to boarding that eastbound. In the brief time since she had set eyes on the big Yankee she had got the hots for him, unexplainable for a working girl like her whose feelings towards her many clients were purely motivated by the size of their bankroll. What he felt about her didn't matter. She wasn't going to just sit here on her sweet ass doing damn all and let that bastard Tod cut Frank to pieces.

Slowly, close eye-watching Tod, she reached out and picked up a metal ashtray from her bedside table and flung it at Tod. Tod yelped in pain as the heavy object struck him on his wounded shoulder. Mouthing obscenities he whirled round to confront Julie, bringing the knife away from Frank's throat. Frank sprang up from the chair like a released spring and grabbed Tod's knife arm by the elbow with one hand, his other hand clamped vice-like on Tod's, trapping the knife in his fist. Then with all his strength, faces inches apart, he forced Tod up against the door.

Planting his right knee in Tod's ample belly he applied the pressure, twisting Tod's knife hand, in over, his grip still preventing the fat man from dropping the blade. Frank grinned wolfishly at Tod. 'I missed you the first time, pilgrim,' he said, 'but you've stolen your last longhorn and beat up your last woman; you're bound for hell.'

Tod's face reddened and the veins in his neck stood out like whipcord as he tried to stop the relentless inching of the knife towards his stomach. Frank saw the flicker of alarm creep into Tod's eyes on hearing his words. He was absolutely certain now that Tod and the other hard-faced men he had seen in the saloon were members of Captain Hardin's gang. He pressed harder. The alarmed look changed into one of pain as he twisted Tod's wounded arm, then into fear and panic as the knife point pricked at his skin. Tod made one last desperate, wildly struggling attempt to heave Frank off him. It was a futile waste of the last few breaths Tod had left to draw on this sweet earth. The knife slipped easily through the belly fat, slicing crossways as Tod's body jerked convulsively in reaction to the thrusting blade.

Tod gave a deep grunt of mortal pain as the knife tore at his insides and the eyes that gazed at Frank were fast emptying of all expression. He fell heavily against Frank, dead, the blood thick and dark welling from his gaping mouth. Frank, his shirt front wet and sticky with Tod's lifeblood, stepped back and let the body slump to the floor to lie in an unmoving untidy heap at his feet.

Swaying slightly Frank turned and faced Julie. Slowly the mad-eyed gargoyle's face changed back into human features as the killing lust drained away from him. Julie, who had wished Tod dead many times over, took one look at the red mess that had once been his stomach then rolled over on to her side and threw up.

Frank looked at her with pity in his eyes. 'Killing, even bastards like Tod who deserve killing, isn't a joyful task, Julie. And in no way does it make a pretty picture. I know, I had two years of killing during the war and it still twists me up inside. I'll get hold of a barkeep to give me a hand to take him away but it will still leave an unpleasant sight in your room.'

Julie sat up and wiped her mouth clean with the back of her hand. She caught a glimpse of herself in the mirror. Reflecting back at her was a fearful old hag's pinch-drawn face. She felt like being sick again. Frank pulled her gently to her feet and holding her at arm's length he said, 'OK, now? You did just fine, if you hadn't made your move when you did more than likely it would have been me lying there.

'Yeah, I'm OK,' Julie replied. 'I'll live I reckon.' She gave Frank a ghost of a smile. 'As long as I don't think about what would have happened to me if it had been you dead on the floor.'

She wanted Frank to hold her tight, regardless of his shirt looking like a slaughterer's apron, to feel his warmth, his strength, to stop the fever-like shakes that were wracking her body. She made the move. 'Hold me Frank,' she softly pleaded. 'Just for a while. I'm still kinda shaky.'

Frank pulled her close, feeling her softness tantalizing warm against him. In spite of a corpse, bleeding all over the floor, and his self-imposed celibacy for Mrs Farrow's sake, it was a hard, physical and emotional battle that Frank fought to stop himself from picking Julie up and laying her across the bed for a short-time of well-earned pleasure, for both of them. Julie sensed what was passing through his mind. She was having the same urges and cravings, and fought against them just as hard. She couldn't give her best, and she wanted to be good for Frank, as long as Tod's carcase was dirtying up the place. She could look at it without wanting to be sick but the fear of him when alive and what could have happened if the son-of-a-bitch had knifed Frank, was still scaring the hell out of her. She drew back her head from Frank's shoulder, sighed, then sweet-smiling said, 'Another time, another place, Frank, we would have been good for each other.'

Frank pulled her back to him and kissed her long

and hard before releasing her. 'We both deserved that, at least, Julie,' he said. 'Now I'll get Tod's body out of here, change my shirt, then come back and ask Mort Dunstan why he allows cut-throats like our late and unlamented friend here freedom of his ranch, and about Captain Hardin. What do you intend doing, Julie? Your room will have to be cleaned up somewhat before you'll be able to use it in comfort.'

Julie told Frank that she was only staying in her room long enough to pack her bags before going down to the rail depot and catching the noon train. She was shaking the dust of Abilene off her shoes. 'I don't want any of Tod's friends thinking that they can take up where he left off, Frank,' she said. 'I couldn't handle any more of that hassle again.'

'You're making a wise move, Julie,' Frank told her. Tod's buddies would undoubtedly ride into town seeking answers for the non-showing up of Tod at the ranch. When they found out he'd been killed Julie would be the first one they'd question. It was definitely better that she should be well away from Abilene; it could save her a lot of grief and pain.

Julie gave Frank a concerned look before speaking. 'Don't let Mort's soft man's look fool you, Frank. He once rode with Colonel Lane's guerillas, before and during the war. They did a lot of killing I hear. So take care.'

Frank gave her a reassuring smile. 'I'll sure have to if you're not staying to back me up. Now it's time I dragged Tod out into the hall and let you get cleaned up and your trunks packed. If I don't see you before you go you take care as well, savvy?'

Mort Dunstan stood behind his bar, eyes focused on the door. He had heard of the manner in which Tod had met his early demise and the barkeep had told him that the sheriff would be paying him a visit and that worried him. He could be coming in just to find out exactly who Tod was for the record and who was prepared to pay to have him buried. But his old marauder highly suspicious nerves wouldn't let him wear that. The new sheriff hadn't seemed a man that would take on a roughneck, an expert knife man, in a life and death struggle over the favours of a two-dollar whore, no matter how pretty she was. When he came to think of it Mr Eberhart didn't need much persuading to take on the sheriff's job and in his opinion only a man wanting to build himself a rep as a shootist, or a man tired of living would take on wearing a peace officer's badge in a wide-open trail-end town. As far as he could judge men Mr Eberhart didn't fit either of those categories. He could be a Federal marshal, a Pinkerton even, trying to track down the boys and had discovered his link with them. He wondered if Tod had talked before he died. Mort shuddered. It was as though somebody had skipped across the grave that was waiting for him a heap sooner than he'd reckoned.

Was he about to lose all that he possessed again? He tried to convince himself that he was getting all worked up for nothing. He knew for a fact that an Apache buck would never have been able to get Tod to talk. It must be only an attack of nerves. But just supposing that things were about to blow up in his face, he thought. This time he was ready and wasn't going down without a fight. He would buy himself sufficient time to grab the cashbox out of the safe and get out of Abilene and start up again somewhere else. That time m'be could only be won by killing the sheriff, if the sheriff was going to push it to a fight. He wasn't too happy about the possibility of gunning down an ex-Union veteran but his support for the Union cause was long-gone. Like Captain Hardin's it died at Appomattox Court House. The only cause left to fight for was his own. Mort eased the big pistol in its sheath on his right hip and shifted the double-barrelled shotgun a few inches nearer the edge of the bar shelf.

When Julie arrived at the rail depot she was surprised to find Ned, one of the Texas Drover's barkeeps, waiting there for the same train.

'I didn't know you were leaving town, Ned,' she said. 'A bit sudden isn't it? I thought you and Mort hit it off?'

'Yeah, we did, Julie,' replied Ned. 'Mort's a good boss. But there's big trouble brewing and I don't want to be around when it starts.'

'What trouble's that?' Julie asked, more for conversational sake than genuine interest. As far as she was aware every day in Abilene in the trailing season was big trouble day for somebody, there was practically a main turnpike leading to Boot Hill nowadays. A Kansas twister could come at any time and suck the whole shebang up to Kingdom Come for all she cared. Her thoughts were still centred on Frank, worrying and fretting about his well-being.

'Mort's all set to gun down the new sheriff, that's all …' Julie heard Ned say. What Ned said next was only a meaningless garble as her mind tried to cope with the sudden shock of Frank walking unknowingly to his death. 'Mort's behind his bar all armed up.' Ned continued. 'He's been

acting queer-like since I told him how Tod met his
end. I don't know what the hell's goin' on but I
don't want to be around when a peace officer ...
where the hell are you goin', Julie?'

'Look after my trunks, Ned, till I get back,' Julie
called over her shoulder. Then with one hand
holding on to her bonnet, the other raising her
skirt high, showing shapely, black stockinged,
fancy-gartered legs, that drew appreciative whoops
from the gawping males along the boardwalks, she
ran along to the sheriff's office to warn Frank of
the danger he was facing.

She tried the office door and found it locked.
'Sweet Jesus,' she breathed, she was too late. Her
stomach knotted up tight as she expected at any
moment to hear the sound of gunfire from the
saloon. Sobbing with frustration Julie picked up
the hem of her skirt again and set off to run the
few blocks to the saloon. Her mind registering only
one thing, the need to find a way to prevent Frank
from ending up like Tod, a lifeless blood-oozing
lump of flesh. She saw the young one-armed
Texan that had been talking to Frank before he
had come up to her room sitting on the porch of
the mayor's general store. Her heart gave a leap,
m'be she had found a way, she thought as she ran
across to him.

'I don't know who you are, mister,' she panted
breathlessly, 'but I saw you talking to Frank, er ...
the sheriff, earlier on. If you are a friend of his he
needs your help right now.'

Phil gave her a fish-eyed look. If the whore knew
that him and Frank were working together who
else did? He also was well aware that the men they
hunted were wary men. He smelt a trap. Whatever

trouble Frank had landed himself in, that is if the little whore was speaking the truth, it wouldn't help him none by going and sticking his head in the same noose.

He knew that there had been some trouble earlier on in the saloon. He'd seen a po-faced, black-garbed man and a young boy bringing out a body from the bar and laying it out on a flat cart before wheeling it past him, heading for some place further along the street. For a few disturbing moments he thought that it was Frank's body the undertaker was dealing with and he vowed that as soon as he'd got to know who was responsible for killing him he would see to it that the son-of-a-bitch paid the price for it. Then Frank himself came out into the street seemingly all in one piece and he sat back in his chair. No doubt when he could, Frank would tell him who it was that had got himself a trip to the undertakers and who sent him there. In the meanwhile he'd stay and watch the saloon and check on the number of hard-faced gents that showed up.

Frank had nodded to him not five minutes ago before he walked into the Drover's saloon for the second time, and as far as could notice there was nothing to see that set the alarm bells ringing in his ears. Now this girl was telling him that Frank was in deep trouble. It definitely had a smell about it. Still keeping his pretence he growled, 'What's m'be happenin' to the big Yankee sheriff don't bother me none, missee; I wouldn't give an ex-blue-belly a drink of water if he was dyin' of thirst. You go and riase a posse or something if you're that keen to help him. I don't even know the sonuvabitch.'

Julie bounced in anger. 'Why you dumb, lying

asshole,' she screeched. 'I saw you talking to him so you must know him! Mort Dunstan's in the saloon all set to shoot him. If you don't want to help him give me that pistol you're carrying and I'll go myself.'

Being called a dumb, lying asshole set Phil's fighting Texas blood to the boil. That accusation coming from a man in any language was "smoking-guns-in-fist" talk but coming from a pretty girl Phil had to eat crow. Besides, he thought he was a lying asshole but dumb he wasn't. The little whore wasn't putting on an act for his benefit. She was really half-scared out of her drawers with worry that Frank was going to get hurt. Why she should be didn't matter although he did quickly opine that the big Yankee must be a fast worker where women were concerned for a mere saloon girl to get so upset about him in the short time he'd been in town. He got to his feet and drew out his pistol.

'Missee,' he said, 'you've done your piece. Just stay well clear, it's man's work now.'

'Balls to you, cowboy,' Julie snapped, still angry with him. 'It's my fight as well, so move ass!'

THIRTEEN

Frank took a quick look round the Texas Drover when he stepped through the doors. As far as he could make out he and Mort were the only ones in the bar, which suited him fine. He wanted it to be a private deal between the two of them. How Mort wanted it played he'd find out soon enough. As he walked across the room he remembered Julie's warning. If Mort's hands, resting on the bar top, as much as twitched he would pull out his pistol and start shooting. Mort wasn't about to catch him off guard like the Texans had.

Frank knew that Mort would be wondering how much he knew about his dealings with Captain Hardin and could end the prying into his affairs right now by gunning him down. He felt the old sickness of fear nibbling away at his insides. He would never make it as a real peace officer. Walking up to a man, expecting at any moment that the man would yank out a pistol and him having to do likewise, scared him. It was bad enough in the heat of battle when blood was running high to kill a man. M'be having to do it in cold blood wasn't his idea of earning an honest day's pay. He stopped short of the bar, gave Mort the once over, then said, 'I reckon you know why

I'm here, Mr Dunstan.'

'I reckon,' replied Mort, flat-voiced. His face had lost its good-living softness, his eyes were hard and watchful. Frank knew that Julie hadn't told him false about Mort Dunstan's hidden toughness.

'I'd like to take you in, Mr Dunstan,' said Frank. 'What Tod told me before he passed over, about your connections with Captain Hardin and his gang of cattle thieves, would make a fair case against you. Me being an officer of the law I could claim that what Tod told me was a death-bed confession for he sure died after he spoke to me about you. I reckon a jury would count that as real convincing evidence, wouldn't you, Mr Dunstan?' Mort favoured him with a slight humourless smile that no way changed his leery-eyed look.

'Now if you were to tell me how many men Captain Hardin has on your ranch, Mr Dunstan,' continued Frank, 'and when he's reckoning to go on his next raid, as far as I'm concerned you can go on being Mr Dunstan the owner of this saloon and keep on making your fortune, or stand for mayor or whatever. You personally didn't steal any of the cattle, and that's all I'm after stopping, that and the killing that goes with it. You have my word on that, Mr Dunstan. Once the gang is broken I'll hand in my badge and ride out of Abilene.'

Mort felt the tension ease out of him. His face lost some of its hawkish lines. Straightening up from the bar he laughed out aloud. 'Tod's death-bed confession my ass, Sheriff. It's a nice try but you're bluffing. I know Tod. He wouldn't talk even if you were to light a fire on his chest. So it will be your word against mine and I know whose say-so a judge would believe. My advice to you,

Sheriff, is to forget all about Captain Hardin and put your mind fully on your job of keeping the peace in Abilene. You'll have all you can handle doing that.' Mort's voice hardened. 'If you're still intent on poking your nose in my business then the mayor could be looking around again for a new sheriff. You'll be keeping Tod company on Boot Hill. And that will be a downright shame because I've got to like you, kid.'

'I was hoping we could do a deal, Mr Dunstan,' Frank said. 'I don't want to have to shoot you and sure as hell I don't hanker after having you plug me but I've personal reasons for seeing that Captain Hardin's put out of business, fast.'

'So?' said Mort almost back to his cheerful welcome-to-the-bar saloon owner's image.

'So,' repeated Frank, 'I go away from here and wait till the trail-hands are in town and well liquored up and I'll put the word round that Mr Mort Dunstan that owns the Texas Drover is behind the men that are stealing their cattle and shooting down their *compadres*. They'll believe me, Mr Dunstan, you can bet on it. You can also bet on it that they'll burn this place down with you in it. Just you think on it a while, Mr Dunstan. I'm not an unreasonable man, I'll give you a coupla hours to make your choice.'

Frank turned from the bar and was halfway to the door; suddenly he heard Julie scream, 'Look out, Frank!'

With nerves strung up tight Frank acted automatically, flinging himself sideways as though Julie had pulled him down with ropes. Then came a single pistol shot instantly drowned by the twin roars of a shotgun discharge. Twisting round on his knees he saw Phil holding a pistol, Julie standing alongside him. Mort lay slumped across the bar. Scattered over him and the bar were the shattered remains of the chandelier that had caught the full blast of the shotgun. Frank swallowed hard as he got shakily to his feet, trying hard not to think of how close he had been to getting all that lead shot in his back.

'That's the second time you've saved my life, Phil,' he said. 'I shouldn't be allowed to walk the streets. I'm getting too old to mix with tough *hombres*.'

'It's the redhead, here, that you should thank,' said Phil. 'She's the one that dragged me here. All I did was point my pistol and pull the trigger.'

Frank gave Julie a weak smile of thanks, his nerves hadn't settled down yet.

'I'm sure glad you didn't take it in your head to catch an earlier train, Julie.' Turning to Phil he said, 'She made the break that allowed me to get the better of Tod, the fella you must have seen being carried out a while back.'

Phil grinned. 'You're durn right, Frank, you country hayseeds shouldn't be wandering about these wild parts without someone holding your hand.'

Frank walked the few steps to the bar. Phil had aimed true; Mort's blood from the big hole at the side of his head was forming a dark, wet pattern on the bartop. Mort had fought his last battle for his twisted views of the Union cause, Frank soberly thought. The sound of the firing had brought men hurrying into the saloon and Frank detailed one of them to recall the undertaker.

'You get the horses saddled up, Phil,' Frank said.

'We're off to pay a visit to Mort's ranch. Better take rations, water, we could be out there for a few days. I'll go, and see the mayor and let him know what's been happening and the lead we've got to the whereabouts of Captain Hardin and his gang.'

'OK,' replied Phil. He bowed low to Julie, taking his hat off in a sweeping exaggerated gesture. 'Miss Julie,' he said. 'I'll walk you back to the depot if you'd allow a dumb, lyin' asshole the honour.'

Julie simpered and fluttered her eyelashes at him. 'Why suh, yuh reb boys sure have a real polite way of asking fur a gal's favours.' In her normal voice she added, 'It's not that I haven't taken a liking to you Frank, I'd like to see more of you, but your eagerness to barge headlong into trouble, like going out to the ranch after what you've just been through would sure turn my hair white if I stayed around in Abilene thinking that m'be for once your luck could run out.'

Phil took hold of her arm. 'Let's go, Red, before he pins a deputy's badge on your chest.'

Frank smiled at them both. 'I'll try and make it to the depot before you leave, Julie. And thanks again for getting that dumb, lying asshole up and running.'

Mayor Bailey listened pop-eyed, jaw dropping lower and lower, frequently voicing a gasped, unbelieving, 'Good Lord' as Frank told him all he knew, or reasonably guessed, about Mort, Tod and the location of the Hardin gang. After Frank had finished speaking he narrow-eyed his new sheriff and in a still-not-quite-believing voice said, 'All this of what you have told me is true? You're sure of it? I just can't really believe that Mort Dunstan is mixed up with a bunch of murderous cattle thieves.

I've known him for years, member of the town committee, preaches at the Meeting House.' Mayor Bailey shook his head and said another 'Good Lord.'

Frank gimlet-eyed him back. 'How many more men do you want bringing in dead to prove it, Mayor? All those men that are not ranch-hands but sleep in the Cross L bunkhouse?'

The mayor snapped his jaws tight shut. His eyes gleamed purposefully, he was convinced at last. Why if he could rope in the Hardin gang, he thought, he was as good as on his way to being State Senator. Opportunity was rapping at the front door and a good politician like himself didn't need it to come and spit in his eye for him to recognize it. True-grit faced he said, 'We'll raise a posse, Sheriff, wire the army to get some their horse-soldier boys to come riding this way. We'll throw a ring round that ranch that a hound dog's fleas couldn't break through.' In his mind's eye he could already see Captain Hardin swinging on the gallows.

'I don't think it wise tactics, Mayor,' said Frank. 'They've got lookouts posted. They'd spot dust trails of a bunch of riders long ways off and the whole gang would scatter, and we'd be having to search for them all over again.'

Mayor Bailey's tough go-get-'em face became ragged at the edges. Opportunity was winging its way past him. He looked at Frank pleadingly. 'Have ... have you got a plan, Sheriff?'

'Yes, Mayor,' replied Frank. 'It's better I go out; I'll take a good man with me and scout out the best way to approach the ranch without being seen, where to position the men to cut off any escape routes. Then I'll come back here, by then you'll have wired the army commander at the fort to have his men standing by, and we'll have a council of war so to speak. I can give the posse their orders, you can ride out and meet the cavalry and explain to them their role in the game.'

'Good thinking, Sheriff, good thinking,' Mayor Bailey said. 'We don't want to go off at half-cock.' He smiled his vote-catching smile as his confidence returned. He was back on the trail to the State Assembly again.

'There is one other thing, Mayor,' said Frank.

Mayor Bailey's smile momentarily flickered then came back full beam. It could only be a slight hiccup in the plans that the kid was going to tell him about he thought. He seemed to have everything else under control. 'Yes?' he asked.

'The reward for bringing Tod in,' said Frank. 'It's a thousand dollars a head for any gang member, dead or alive, I believe. I know that wearing a sheriff's badge prevents me from claiming the bounty, but the citizen who put me on to Tod and played a major part in bringing him to where he is now on a board in the undertaker's parlour deserves it.'

'So he shall, Sheriff, so he shall. By golly I'll see to it personally,' Mayor Bailey blurted out in a relieved, expansive frame of mind. 'Once Tod has been definitely indentified as being a member of the gang and you fill in all the legal papers, he'll be entitled to the reward. Of course it might take a few weeks, these things have to go through the proper channels, but he'll get it.'

'This er, citizen, is a girl, Mayor,' Frank said lamely. 'A saloon girl in the Texas Drover. She insists that she wants the reward money paying over now.'

Mayor Bailey gave a derisive laugh. 'It can't be done, Sheriff. We can't hand out a thousand dollars without first checking that the dead man Tod, was one of Captain Hardin's gang. Why we'd have Abilene full of dead bodies and people claiming that they were outlaws with prices on their heads. You just explain that to her. I'm sure she'll understand and won't mind waiting a while for the reward.'

'I did tell her that, Mayor,' Frank replied. 'But she wasn't having any of it. She said she wanted her due now, she wants to get out of town, or she'd blab to all clients what she knows. The Texans, as you well know, Mayor, are wild tempestuous boys and that news would set them high-tailing it to round up the captain themselves so that they can put a rope collar round his neck. That would sure ruin our plan to sneak up and grab the whole gang.'

Mayor Bailey knew when he was between a rock and a hard place, knew when it was time to bend a little or lose all. Showing a bold, resolute face he pulled out his watch and glanced at the time then said, 'The bank's open now; I'll go and draw out a thousand dollars on a personal cheque. For once, Sheriff, we needn't wait till the paper work is complete.'

Julie heard the strident clanging of the eastbound flyer's bell and saw the black plume of its stack smoke reaching into the sky beyond the curve in the track. She looked over her shoulder, back towards the town, but could see no sign of Frank. She felt a pang of disappointment. He had promised and she felt that he had really meant it.

Julie put down the reason that Frank hadn't made it to the depot to see her off was that the old windbag that passed himself off as Mayor of Abilene had kept him talking.

The train came rattling into view. Julie got to her feet and ruefully shrugged her shoulders. Life was full of hard knocks and dashed hopes, as if she didn't damn well know that all ready, she bitterly thought. She reached down for her bags as the flyer drew up at the depot. Frank beat her to it. Julie grinned. 'You cut it fine, you big Yankee ploughboy.'

'Yeah, I know,' replied Frank. 'But the business with the mayor took a mite longer than I reckoned. There's something I want to tell you, Julie, so I'll have to make it quick.'

'You don't have to, Frank. The engineer loads up with wood, tops his boiler up with water here. Abilene is a twenty minute halt. You've got plenty time to say what you've got on your mind.'

'Good,' said Frank. And taking hold of Julie's arm he led her to the rear of a depot shack.

More than Julie's female curiosity was aroused. Surely Frank wasn't going to have her here and now in the brush alongside the shack like some Apache buck mounting his squaw she thought. By golly if she hadn't been wearing her best dress and her fine new black silk stockings she would have dragged him into the brush and to hell with catching the train. Blood pounding she waited for what Frank had to tell her.

Frank waited till the few passengers for the train had boarded before he placed the envelope containing the reward money in Julie's hand. 'That's the bounty money for Tod's scalp,' he said.

'A thousand dollars. I squeezed it out of the mayor a bit faster than he's allowed to legally. It's yours, you earned it.'

For once in her life Julie was lost for words. She could only gaze wide-eyed with surprise at the weighty envelope.

Frank gently raised up her head and looked at her straight in the eyes. 'Speaking as a Dutch uncle,' he said, 'why don't you use the money as a grubstake for setting yourself up in some small business? It'll bring you a better life than being a saloon girl will. You won't have assholes like Tod pawing over you. I hope I'm not speaking out of turn, Julie, but it's the least I can do for you, the money and the advice. You gave me back my life, twice over, I am beholden to you.'

Julie lowered her head again. She didn't dare look Frank in the eyes or the tears she was holding back would come flooding out. And whoever heard of a whore crying her head off in public like a love-sick kid? Then philosophically she told herself that she hadn't a snowball's chance in hell of netting in Frank. It had all been wishful thinking on her part. She hadn't got the jackpot but she'd got herself a good second prize, the thousand dollars, more money than she could ever hope to earn peddling her ass. Somehow she got a grip on her emotions and looked up at Frank. 'I had a fancy idea once of running my own business if ever I got hold of some real cash. Now I might just do that.' She put her arms round Frank's neck and pulled his head down to hers and kissed him, long and sweet.

She drew back and said, 'It's no good me speaking like a Dutch aunt by telling you not to go on your foolhardy trip to Mort's ranch because I can recognize a stubborn asshole when I see one and you'd only give me that crap about a man's gotta do what a man's gotta do. So all I can say is take care, likewise the Texan kid, so a certain ex-redhead whore can sleep peacefully at night in her bed.' Julie suddenly grabbed her bags and almost ran to the flyer, holding her tears back no longer.

Frank looked for her as the train pulled out but couldn't see her. If there had been time he would have liked to thank her more but as it was he felt that he had done right by her, paid his debt to her. What he owed to Mrs Farrow couldn't be paid off so easy. Only blood, not currency, would settle that debt. Preferably Captain Hardin's to his. He walked across to the livery barn, praying that the luck he and Phil were having would still hold up.

'Tod hasn't showed up, Captain,' said Sergeant Kegg. 'And I have to report that Ned, when he was on lookout duty last night, fired at something he thought he heard. He searched the area at first light but couldn't find anything and the ground's too hard to show sign. I didn't see any reason to wake you, Captain but I did double the guards just in case Ned heard right.'

Captain Hardin turned away from gazing out of the window across the silent plain and faced his sergeant. 'One man missing, another firing at shadows. What do you make of it, Sergeant?'

'I know Tod has a woman in Abilene that he craves for but I've never known him miss a roll call. And Ned ain't a man that's got a nervous trigger-finger.'

'My thoughts exactly, Sergeant,' said Captain Hardin. 'Tod being missing and Ned's shooting could be just a coincidence but I don't think so. I may be wrong but we can't take chances. It looks damn quiet and peaceful out there but there could be one helluva storm getting set to blow up. Have the men ready to move out in an hour's time, Sergeant.' Captain Hardin's eyes gleamed in a wild faraway look and his lips drew back like a wolf contemplating his next meal. 'The next raid we make will be in the rebs' own backyard, Sergeant, Texas ...'

FOURTEEN

'We're getting close to where I was fired at, Frank,' said Phil a little apprehensively. 'Do you think it's wise to be parading along putting ourselves up as clear targets? He could be drawin' a bead on us right now with a long gun and we'd be too late to do anything about it.'

Smiling, Frank said, 'For a young kid you worry a lot, Phil. This is a main trail and hazarding a guess, across open country, we've every right to be here. If the lookout is still posted you can bet on it that he has orders to ignore the occasional rider that uses the trail. The captain won't want to attract undue attention to this section of territory by shooting down any rider that happens to come along. A big bunch of hard-riding men wouldn't get by so easy. But that doesn't mean we can poke our noses around the ranch without getting close-eyed challenged. So we'll just cast a quick glance at it as we pass by then swing round and come on to it by the back door.' In spite of his confident assessment of the way he reckoned the captain would be thinking, he knew he was going up against a man who acted and thought a great deal faster than most or he would have been long since dead; not to tempt providence too far he had taken off his sheriff's badge. The sight of a tin star would set trigger-fingers taking up the first pressure on Colts and Winchesters.

Several more minutes' ride and the main ranch buildings of the Cross L came into view, set back some three hundred yards at the head of a track that forked eastwards from the main trail.

Frank drew up his horse, Phil following suit. 'OK, Phil,' he said. 'I'll step down and start checking my saddle just to fool anyone that could be watching us. You give the place a good look over. Find out if there's a way we can get closer without being seen. But stay mounted and make it casual like, remember we're supposed to be a couple of drifters.'

Frank waited, dry-throated, as he fiddled with the saddle straps, expecting at any moment to see tough-visaged men holding guns step out on to the trail and ask them their business. It was with some relief that he heard Phil say.

'I've seen all I want, Frank, there ain't a big bunch of men there. I've spotted six men, there's m'be another in the big house plus the cook, that's about a normal crew for a ranch this size. If the captain and his boys were here I'd expect to see a lot more horse flesh in the corral. I've found a spot where we can get real close in if you want to.'

'Damnit,' said Frank as he swung back on to his saddle. He knew that he'd been right about Captain Hardin using the ranch as his hole-up. Mort wouldn't have laid his life on the line otherwise. All that must have happened was that the Captain had pulled up stakes and ridden out on another raid. But in God's name where, he frantically thought. Captain Hardin and his gang on the loose with the Double Star on the trail heading north by now gave him the shakes.

Grim-faced he said, 'Let's go in Phil and start asking questions and getting quick answers.' He kneed his horse forward into a canter.

They left their mounts well hidden in a grab of timber and brush to the north of the ranch. Keeping crouched down they indianed up on the ranch by way of a narrow dried-out wash. Unobserved they came out of the wash and dropped behind a fold in the ground, some twenty feet away from a ranch-hand fixing some fencing, the rest of the ranch crew being well scattered doing chores on the far side of the ranch.

'You go, Phil,' Frank whispered. 'I'll stay and cover you. If trouble comes I've got two good hands to use.' Phil was already belly-crawling towards the unsuspecting ranch-hand.

The ranch-hand heard the ominous click of a pistol hammer being thumbed back, his hammer hand froze in mid-air. He made to turn but suddenly stopped when he heard a voice say, 'Don't turn around, just act naturally. Try to call out and I'll blow your head clean off.' he knew that the owner of the voice meant it.

'I ain't got the time for small talk, amigo,' Phil said. 'So I'll get straight to the point. Where are Captain Hardin and his boys bound for?'

In spite of the warning the ranch-hand risked a look over his shoulder. He saw a mean-faced one-eyed kid holding a big pistol dead centre on him then wished he hadn't. He quickly looked to his front again.

'I don't know what you're talkin' about, mister,' the ranch-hand said, trying to bluff it out. 'Ain't no

Captain what's-his-name here. Never even heard
of the guy. There's only the regular crew on the
spread, eight of us, counting the cook over there in
the kitchen.'

'Well, well, what do you know,' Phil said. 'I've
met the only asshole in the whole of Kansas that
ain't heard of Captain Hardin and his gang of "Red
Leg" cattle thieves. Now I'll tell you what you really
don't know; your boss, Mort, is dead, so's Tod.' Phil
grinned as he saw the ranch-hand's head jerk on
hearing that news. 'Back on the trail there are a
bunch of Texans. They've ridden out here to see
the captain and his boys dance under a hangin'
tree. They'll be right disappointed that the captain
ain't here especially when they're all worked up for
a hangin'. And west Texas *hombres* are like spoilt
kids if they don't get what they've set their minds
on.' Phil saw the ranch-hand shuffle his feet
nervously in the dirt. 'In fact they'll be so right put
out that they're liable to hang every living thing on
this ranch, cows, goats, sheep, chickens. That is
after they've strung you and your *compadres* up.
Now cut out the crap and tell where Captain
Hardin is and I might stop the boys from hangin'
you.'

The ranch-hand wheeled round, face working
with fear. 'I ain't one of the gang, mister, I'm just a
ranch-hand. The captain and his boys rode out
about an hour ago.'

'Where?' asked Phil.

'I don't know exactly,' the man replied. Seeing
Phil's disbelieving look and the pistol steadying on
him again he screamed, 'Honest I don't! All I know
is what he told his boys, they were headin' for
below the Red, into Texas. What cattle they lift

they'll move along the old cattle trail eastwards to
Sedalia, Missouri. The whole sixteen of them rode
off. And that's all I know.'

'Thanks, mister, for being so cooperative,' said
Phil. 'Don't go and spoil it all by goin' for your gun
when I turn my back. There's a Winchester laid on
you not twenty feet away.' Phil raised his voice.
'Show yourself, Frank!' Frank got to his feet
holding the rifle up to his shoulder. Phil grinned at
the twitchy-faced ranch-hand. 'You just carry on
doin' your chores, though I don't know who's goin'
to pay your wages what with Mort getting himself
killed. *Adios, amigo.*' He turned and walked back to
Frank, keeping well clear of the aimed Winchester
in case the ranch-hand got an attack of heroics and
tried his luck.

Frank couldn't remember walking back to his
horse. Phil telling him about Captain Hardin's
plans for operating in Texas had sent his mind into
a whirling jumble of frightening despondent
thoughts. Being short-handed, Sam and the boys
were already at risk once they crossed into the
Nations. Sam would be half expecting an attack
and try to keep the hands on the alert to meet it if it
came. A raid on Texas territory would catch him
wrong-footed. The Double Star would have no
chance at all. Then there was Mrs Farrow.
Thinking of how she could end up caught in the
middle of a gun battle, lying torn and bloodied on
the plain, sent Frank's spirits down low. What price
his covenant then?

Phil watched all that was passing through Frank's
mind, reflected in his face, hard-planed with wild
but not seeing eyes, but kept quiet. *Compadres* or
not he wasn't about to break into his thoughts by

asking him what the next moves were. Right now he was eyeballing a short-fused *hombre,* a wrong word would have him pulling out his gun. He knew that Frank had a lot more plaguing his insides than mere loyalty to the Double Star and Mrs Farrow. What was driving the Yankee on was his promise made to the dead Captain Farrow back at Chickamaugo to look out for his widow. If he failed to do that, even through no fault of his own like it looked right now by the raiders slipping through their fingers, the whole reason for Frank's living was gone. Frank Eberhart, Phil concluded, could turn into a real mean-assed son-of-a-bitch. So till Frank sorted himself out he'd keep his lips buttoned up tight.

By the time Frank remounted he could put the frightening picture images of Mrs Farrow lying dead on the plains at the back of his mind. His natural stubborness that pulled him through the bad times during the war wouldn't let him stay down long. He hadn't lost the war yet; it was time for serious thinking.

'This is what we do, Phil,' he said. 'We go back to Abilene, hand in my badge, tell the mayor the situation here. Ask him to wire the army HQ in north Texas to have patrols sent out along the Texas, Nations border. I'm not expecting that they'll corner the captain unless they get real lucky but we'll have done our duty. Then you and me, Phil, go back down the Chisholm Trail as fast as we can without killing our horses till we meet the Double Star herd, and m'be get us some help on the way. Luke Dolan should supply that if his word is good.'

'Will we be in time, Frank,' Phil asked anxiously. 'He's got a few hours lead on us.'

'I think so, Phil,' replied Frank. 'He won't be travelling on the main trails, too open for him. He'll have to use the time-wasting back trails. It will be a long ride for him for him to reach where he wants to be.' Frank, feeling more hopeful smiled at Phil. 'OK, reb, let's go and tell Mayor Bailey that he needs a new sheriff and his grand hopes of catching Captain Hardin and the whole of his gang have fallen through. That, I reckon, should cheer him up no end.'

FIFTEEN

'Well I'll be durned,' exclaimed Luke Dolan as Frank and Phil rode into the Bar X camp. 'If you boys will keep on visiting me I'll have to add you on to the payroll.'

His face quickly lost its good humoured look when Frank related as briefly as possible the events that had taken place in Abilene and the latest intelligence regarding Captain Hardin and his gang and his urgent need for men to protect the Double Star's trail herd.

Luke Dolan gave a low whistle of astonishment after Frank had finished talking.

'You boys don't let the grass grow under your feet, that's for sure.' The Bar X foreman did some rapid calculations. 'I can spare you five men, Mr Eberhart, good men to be at your side in a tight corner.'

'Thanks, Mr Dolan,' said Frank. 'They'll do just fine.'

'Ok, then,' said Luke Dolan. 'Grab yourself a bite to eat and some coffee, I'll pick the men and extra mounts for you all as well.'

When they were mounted up and ready to ride Luke Dolan spoke to a tall, lantern-jawed trail-hand. 'I know that all your brothers got kilt by

the blue-bellies during the war, Cliff, but Mr
Eberhart there is the man in charge, we owe him
that, *comprende?* I'm relying on you to keep the rest
of the boys in line. There's another thing you can
do, Cliff, should help you out some more, Mr
Eberhart. Lew Cassidy's herd is trailin' behind us,
somewhere back of him is old man Lewis's beef.
You can ask them, Cliff, for as many men as they
can give you. Tell them what Mr Eberhart's told me
that Captain Hardin is way back in Texas. You can
also tell them that if they don't come up with the
men they can kiss that poker game the three of us
a'goin' to have in Abilene goodbye. Away you go,
boys, and good luck.'

By the time they raised the Red River Frank had
a small army under his command. He had picked
up another seven men from the two ranchers that
Luke Dolan had mentioned; twelve tough, hard-
riding men, most of them veterans of the
hell-raising horse soldier outfits of Stonewall
Jackson and Nathen Bedford Forest's brigades;
man for man more than a match for Captain
Hardin and his back-shooting "Red Legs." With
the added strength the Double Star could deter the
captain from attacking them. If he did Frank had
no doubts that they would whip him. The only
doubts he did have was that they could be too late,
that the captain had already shown his hand. If
they were, Frank told himself he'd catch up with
the sons-of-bitches on the Sedalia trail and see
them all hung or shot.

A single rider appeared from over a ridge ahead
of them, saw them then pulling his mount up
sharp, turned to ride back over the rise. Phil pulled
out his pistol and fired three rapid shots in the air.

Grinning widely at Frank he said, 'It's Waco! I can smell the old goat from here!'

Waco turned his horse round again and came riding towards them. Frank let out a whoop of sheer joy. Next to Mrs Farrow, when he saw her once more, Waco's dour visage, creased now in an unaccustomed smile, was the most beautiful sight he had seen since leaving Abilene. Gone for good were his worries and fears about what could have happened to Isobel. Captain Hardin could never harm her now.

If Sam Ford had not been a tough, hard, straw-boss when Waco rode into camp with Frank and Phil at the head of the small column of riders he would have shed real womanish tears. As it was his eyes only moisted over. But he was too choked up emotionally with relief and delight at the sight of the extra men that he could do no more than shake Frank and Phil's hands when they dismounted and nod his thanks, and say to Frank, 'Mrs Farrow's down at the crick.'

The herd was bedded down north of a small but water-filled creek. The cook's wagon was perched on the rim of the wash and at the foot of the shallow bank Isobel Farrow was busy washing some of her clothes. Something made her look up and she saw Frank standing at the wagon. Being a woman who had spent sleepless nights worrying herself sick about the man she knew she loved yet had not told him so, or never maybe would be able to tell him for he would be dead like her first love, she didn't have any inhibitions in showing her heartfelt relief at seeing Frank returning alive. She dropped the garment she was washing and ran to Frank sobbing loudly and flung herself into his open arms.

Frank held her close, feeling ten feet tall. Her action of coming to him told him more than words could how she felt towards him, saved him the tongue-tied embarrassment of trying to explain to her his own feelings about their future together. Frank knew that part of Isobel would still reach out to Captain Farrow. He wouldn't want to begrudge her those memories. Isobel held enough love for both of them and Captain Farrow had been a man who could hold a woman's love even after death. He could live with that. They clung together for a while, not speaking, enjoying the pleasure of their embracing before walking back to the camp holding hands as though they had been "walking out" regularly.

Sam had seen the extra hands fed, posted some of them as night riders on the herd to double up with his own crew. Two, both 'breeds, with the keenness of sight and hearing of their Indian fathers, he sent out as left-hand and right-hand loop men to patrol the whole camp. They would give him that few extra minutes' warning if trouble came, the difference between life or death for the Double Star crew. The rest of the men were sitting round the fire talking and smoking. Sam smiled fatherly as Frank and Isobel stepped into the firelight. The boss was going to get the full happiness she missed out on all these years, the peace of mind she deserved.

Isobel let go of Frank's hand. 'You go and join them, Frank, I've a lot to do yet and I'd like an early night.' She sweet-smiled Frank. 'I haven't been sleeping so well lately.'

Frank squatted down in the circle of men at the fire and rolled himself a making. As he was lighting it Sam Ford said, 'Cliff and some of his boys think that we should take on the captain and his bunch now that we're more or less equal in numbers. Cliff here has sort of a plan. He reckons to know where Captain Hardin will show up. But I hear that Luke Dolan made you the boss so it's up to you whether or not we go along with Cliff's scheme.'

'What do you think of tangling with the captain, Sam?' Frank said.

'I think that the captain has had a long enough run,' Sam answered. 'And this could be the best chance we trail-hands have of going and getting him and his boys and putting them away permanently.'

Frank saw the unspoken words in Sam's look ... "As long as Mrs Farrow doesn't get hurt," Frank turned to the lean-faced Cliff. 'OK, Cliff tell me about this plan of yours, and why you are so sure that Captain Hardin will come out of those far hills where you say so.'

Cliff told him of how in his younger, wilder days, he ran with a bunch of penny-ante horse and cattle thieves across this very piece of territory. He'd been chased over it by marshals' posses and Texas Rangers so many times that he was familiar with every rock and blade of grass on it. The only good trail through the hills leading south from the Nations came out on the flat not two miles south from where they were sitting right now. There were other trails in the back country but they led deeper into Texas or petered out long ways back. His plan was to set up an ambush to catch the gang as they came down through the last pass.

'Why would the captain take it in his head to come out into the open from that particular trail,

Cliff?' Frank asked. 'He might be intendin' to ride deeper into Texas to do his stealing.'

Cliff gave him a horse-tooth grin. 'Less than a day's trailin' ahead, Mr Eberhart, is the cut-off to the cattle trail that leads all the way to Sedalia. According to Phil that's where the captain is goin' to shin his stolen beef from. The way I figure it the captain will want to get off the Chisholm Trail as fast as he can, he'll want a clear run for his cattle. Seeing this herd so near the road he intends taking should pull him out of those hills even if he was thinking of riding all the way to El Paso to steal Texas beef.'

Frank thought hard about what Cliff had told him. His reasoning made sense. The captain couldn't be all that far behind on the trail. But he didn't like the ambush. The captain could slip by it, be at the herd before the ambush party could get back. M'be he wouldn't get away with stealing any of the cattle but he could do some killing. And like Sam in no way was he going to put Isobel's life in jeopardy. Nailing Captain Hardin and his whole gang wasn't worth that risk.

'OK, Cliff,' Frank said. 'We'll trail our coat-tails for the captain but only for a day or we'll have some other herd sniffing up our asses. And Mrs Farrow wants to get her beef to Abilene before the longhorns drop in price.' He favoured Cliff with an icy smile. 'And we don't go for the captain, we draw the sonuvabitch on to us right here in the open.' Frank pointed out into the dark. 'We'll make that the killing ground. And we do it like this ...'

Before first light all the men that Frank had brought with him were fed and allocated their specific tasks. Five men, and Mrs Farrow, would hide up in the timber along the creek. If an attack came they would ride out and cut off the captain's retreat. All but one of them that is. He would stay behind, Frank had beady-eyed insisted, to protect Mrs Farrow. The regular Double Star crew would drive the herd a mile or so along the trail, far enough for the creek not to be used as a covered approach by the gang. Then the front axle of the cook's wagon would snap, taking all the crew excepting the two hands riding the herd to repair it. That's the way Captain Hardin would see it. The contents of the wagon strewn all over the ground, a bunch of men grouped round working on the broken part. What he wouldn't see, or suspect, Frank fervently hoped, was himself and five men inside the wagon nursing Winchester repeating rifles. Frank gave the two 'breeds free rein. Their fathers' blood would tell them the best way to play their part in any fight.

Thinking it over again Frank reckoned that they were as ready as they could be for any eventuality. All it wanted was the captain to show up and take the bait. If he didn't all that they had lost was a day's trailing. Cliff thought that it was a plan worthy of General Nat Forest at his sneakiest. That comment pleased Frank more than somewhat. A battle was halfway to being won if the man in charge had the confidence of the men who were going to fight it for him. He asked Cliff if he and the boys would not think it amiss of him if he wore his Union army jacket, that the sight of a blue-belly uniform would not raise hackles or stir up bitter, not-so-deeply-buried memories. He told Cliff that foolish as it sounded the jacket he felt was some sort of a talisman, that wearing it had pulled him through safely at Chickamaugo and m'be its good luck could see him through this little skirmish, if it came to one. A po-faced Cliff had replied that he would tell the boys that the blue-bellies they might be shooting at were outside the wagon, not rubbing shoulders with them.

It had been a long, sweaty ball-aching wait for the men in the cook's wagon and for the men stretching out their imaginary work repairing an axle that wasn't broken. They couldn't drop their pretence for one second. For all they knew they could have been spied on by Captain Hardin all morning. One after twelve the fish was seen to be nibbling. Chris, one of the men riding the herd, cantered slowly back to the cook's wagon. Dismounting he poured himself out a mug of coffee then walked over to the men working on the axle.

'I've seen a flash of light, Frank,' he said, just loud enough for the men in the wagon to hear. 'Away to the left of the herd, no more than half a mile away. Could be some *hombre* giving us a looksee with army glasses.' Tossing the dregs of his coffee away Chris got astride his horse again and rode just as casually back to the herd. Frank, standing at the mouth of the wagon, heard a stirring behind as the men stretched their limbs. He heard the double snicks of Winchester cocking levers being worked. 'OK, boys, it looks like party time is upon us. Don't cut loose till I give the word, let them come in real close, we want them all.'

The men working on the axle stopped what they were doing and strolled back to the camp fire and the concealed weapon pits with rifles lying handy.

Captain Hardin put his glasses back in their case.

He had been taking his last look at the camp he had first noticed from the high ground. He had thought of coming on them from the rear, by way of the creek that snaked its way across the plains. But that would take time and time was something he felt he was running out of. Someone, the law or the Pinkertons, had trailed him to Mort's ranch. The same people could be right now haring along his back trail. The few men he saw clustered around the camp were easy meat. He would attack in the time-honoured method of the raiders, get in as close as they could undetected then charge in shooting.

Captain Hardin raised a white-gloved hand and his men swung on to their horses. Frank, peering round the arched corner of the wagon, saw a ragged line of riders suddenly appear as though the ground had sprouted them up, then became a moving semicircle arc as they rode towards the camp. The Double Star crew dropped down into their trenches and began to fire at the raiders, picking one or two of them off. It didn't stop the charge. The gang expected to meet retaliation fire for a minute or so before they stomped the riflemen into the ground.

Frank waited a few more gut-churning seconds before yelling, 'OK, boys! Let the sonsuvbitches have it!'

The wagon tarp was slashed open and the Winchesters opened up in one concerted, nonstop magazine-emptying barrage. The raiders were swept off their horses as though some great unseen blade had passed through them. The line swayed then broke. Those that were still upright in their saddles headed back along the way they had come.

Frank saw dust trails closing in on them from either flank. His ambush party and the 'breeds. Two of the raiders, Captain Hardin and Sergeant Kegg, raised the dust as they rode towards the creek and its sheltering trees.

Frank cursed and jumped out of the wagon and on to the nearest horse and gave chase, praying that Isobel had hidden herself well. He exchanged shots with the raider riding behind the man dressed up in a Union officer's uniform, realising with grim satisfaction that it could only be Captain Hardin. A lucky shot hit the raider's horse causing it to stumble and throw its rider to the ground. Frank swerved his horse towards him and bringing his gun hand over his horse's neck coldly and dispassionately thumbed off a Colt-load at him as he struggled on to his feet.

Sergeant Kegg landed hard, knocking all the wind out of him. Still half dazed by the fall he got groggily to his feet. Then he saw a big horseman wearing a Union army tunic almost on top of him aiming a pistol at his head. He saw its flash then felt a split second of intense pain before the whole world blew up in his face and the impact of the heavy ball flung him back to the ground, the sound of the shot echoing silently in a dead man's ears.

Frank caught a glimpse of Captain Hardin before he was swallowed up by the trees and brush. Thinking only of Isobel and the danger she could be in with a wild kill-crazy man like the captain loose in the woods his heel dug his horse's ribs and charged in after him. Only when the trees and the undergrowth closed in on him did Frank doubt the wisdom of barging into what easily could turn out to be a death-trap for him. But it was too late to worry about that now. He slipped off his horse, reloaded his pistol in all its chambers, and proceeded through the timber on foot, as slowly and quietly as he could knowing that from any tree or clump of brush he could be shot down dead. He began to shiver and his nerve ends ached. He hadn't managed yet to lay to rest the terrible experiences he had gone through at Chickamaugo.

He reached the lip of the bank of the creek and still hadn't heard or seen any signs of the captain. A noise to his left caused him to swing sharply round, pistol hammer at full cock. Captain Hardin's horse stepped into view, with no rider on its back. Frank's insides shrivelled up. Any minute he would feel the terrible tearing pain of a bullet hitting him. The captain had him by the balls. He was as good as dead. Before he could think of somewhere he could dive to in a wild attempt to get out of the gun sights of a man he couldn't guess in which direction he was watching him from a voice said, 'This way, Sergeant. And drop your pistol or I'll kill you out of hand.'

Frank slowly turned his head. Captain Hardin stood on the opposite bank, a pistol held at arm's length pointing at him. Frank dropped his gun to the ground.

'I want to see what sort of a man it is that wears the Union blue and fights alongside rebel scum.' The captain's face worked in anger. 'I take it, Sergeant, that you're entitled to wear that tunic?'

Frank's desperate will to live overcame his fear. Every second he delayed the captain from pulling that trigger was another second of life he had won for himself and m'be that miracle he was praying like hell for would happen.

'I wore it with honour at Chickamaugo Creek, serving under General Grant, Captain,' Frank said, straight-eyeing the captain. 'I didn't expect to be fired at by a man that favoured the same cause and wears the same blue.'

Frank saw the pistol lower slightly and a hesitant, confused look flashed across the captain's face. Then the pistol lifted and steadied and the face hardened as the captain regained control of himself.

'The Union I fought for no longer exists, Sergeant,' he said, loud-voiced as a street-corner agitator. 'The men in Washington betrayed the cause, gave in to the slavers; And you, Sergeant, by siding with these Texan rebels are part of that betrayal!' Captain Hardin brought up his other hand to steady the pistol and Frank knew that he had lost out. The captain was quite mad and what little chance he'd had pleading that they had both fought on the same side during the war had only prolonged his life the time it had taken to say it. Frank got set to jump into the creek, anything, but standing here like a dumb ox waiting for the slaughterer.

Isobel waited in the trees as anxious as the trail-hands, with one big difference. They were eager for Captain Hardin and his gang to show up, as keen as hound dogs for the chase, to get another chance to kill Unionists: she praying that the captain was across at the other side of Texas so that there would be no more shooting, no more killing. The Double Star crew weren't just ranch-hands on a payroll. Sam, Phil, Chris, Charlie, even old Waco were family. They had all played a part in building

up the ranch. And Frank; Isobel, in spite of her
fears, smiled softly, he was something special. She
hoped to God he stayed alive so that she could
prove physically just how much she had grown to
love him.

At the sound of the firing from the direction of
the camp Isobel's stomach knotted up into a hard
ball of pain. She saw the trail-hands grinning at
each other as they mounted up as though they
were riding off to a barn dance, not to face possible
death. The man detailed to stay behind and guard
her wasn't sharing in the general excitement. He
had a dour, left-out-of-it look on his face.

'There's no need for you to stay and watch over
me,' Isobel told him. 'I have a rifle and know how
to use it. I'll be quite safe here.'

'But Mr Eberhart told us that one of us must stay
with you,' the trail-hand replied.

'There're no buts about it,' Isobel said sharply.
'Mr Eberhart is only my cook, I'm the boss of the
Double Star. Every rifle will be needed at the camp.
Yours will be wasted sitting down here with me.'

'OK, boss lady,' the trail-hand said as he leapt on
to his horse. He pulled his Winchester out of its
loop and yelled, 'OK, fellas, let's go and get a
blue-belly apiece!'

The firing had almost died away when Isobel
heard thrashing in the brush behind her. She stood
up, gripping the rifle tightly, wishing a little that
she had not ordered her guard away. She heard
more snapping of branches and she caught a
glimpse of Frank through the trees. The brush was
.too thick for her to make her way directly to him so
she ran down the slope towards the creek to see if
there was a clearer path at the water's edge and saw

a man wearing a Union officer's uniform standing on the far bank holding a pistol on Frank. She could not have saved her first husband's life but she had the chance to save the life of the man she wanted for her second husband. Controlling her nerves, having never before deliberately contemplated killing a man, she brought up her rifle and took careful aim.

Frank heard a rifle crack to his right and the captain staggered back a pace, his shattered gun arm dropping uselessly by his side, his mad-eyed expression changing into one of painful surprise. The utter relief at being drawn back from the brink of the grave sent the adrenalin coursing through Frank's body. The miracle had happened. In one sweeping movement he scooped up his pistol from the ground and fanned off the whole six loads at the captain. He didn't know how many of them hit his target but he saw the captain twist round as if trying to dodge the hail of bullets then slowly fold at the middle to overbalance and slip head-first into the creek, to be quickly carried away by the fast flowing current. Isobel lowered her rifle and ran along the creek bank to Frank.

Sam saw Isobel give Frank his break by wounding the captain. He wasn't a religious man: he fell out with that way of thinking the night the Indians took away his wife and child, but he reckoned that there must be someone or something to have pre-ordained that first Captain Farrow then Mrs Farrow had saved Frank's life. It was as the Indians believed that a man's whole life was written out like some book and all he had to do was to play it out. It had been one hell of a bloody story, stretching from the slaughter at Chickamaugo to the killings along this pissy little creek in Texas for Frank to act out before becoming the future boss of the Double Star. He watched Frank and Mrs Farrow embracing then he said to Phil, standing beside him, 'How does having a blue-belly for a boss grab you, kid?'

Phil grinned. 'As long as he don't put Waco back in the cookhouse the big Yankee will do for me.'